PENGUIN CLASSICS

The Late Monsieur Gallet

'I love reading Simenon. He makes me think of Chekhov'
William Faulkner

'A truly wonderful writer . . . marvellously readable – lucid,
simple, absolutely in tune with the world he creates'

Muriel Spark

'Few writers have ever conveyed with such a sure touch, the
bleakness of human life'   A. N. Wilson

'One of the greatest writers of the twentieth century . . .
Simenon was unequalled at making us look inside, though
the ability was masked by his brilliance at absorbing us
obsessively in his stories'   *Guardian*

'A novelist who entered his fictional world as if he were part
of it'   Peter Ackroyd

'The greatest of all, the most genuine novelist we have had in
literature'   André Gide

'Superb . . . The most addictive of writers . . . A unique teller
of tales'   *Observer*

'The mysteries of the human personality are revealed in all
their disconcerting complexity'   Anita Brookner

'A writer who, more than any other crime novelist, combined
a high literary reputation with popular appeal'   P. D. James

'A supreme writer . . . Unforgettable vividness'   *Independent*

'Compelling, remorseless, brilliant'   John Gray

'Extraordinary masterpieces of the twentieth century'

John Banville

ABOUT THE AUTHOR

Georges Simenon was born on 12 February 1903 in Liège, Belgium, and died in 1989 in Lausanne, Switzerland, where he had lived for the latter part of his life. He published seventy-five novels and twenty-eight short stories featuring Inspector Maigret.

The Late Monsieur Gallet was the first Maigret novel to be published in book form. The series was launched in February 1931 with a lavish themed party, the 'Anthropometric Ball', complete with invitations in the form of police record cards and fake policemen stationed at the entrance.

Penguin is publishing the entire series of Maigret novels.

GEORGES SIMENON

The Late Monsieur Gallet

Translated by ANTHEA BELL

PENGUIN BOOKS

PENGUIN CLASSICS

UK | USA | Canada | Ireland | Australia
India | New Zealand | South Africa

Penguin Books is part of the Penguin Random House group of companies
whose addresses can be found at global.penguinrandomhouse.com.

Penguin
Random House
UK

First published in French as *M. Gallet décédé* by Fayard 1931
This translation first published 2013

020

Typeset in Dante by Palimpsest Book Production Ltd, Falkirk, Stirlingshire
Printed and bound in Great Britain by Clays Ltd, Elcograf S.p.A.

ISBN: 978–0–141–39337–7

www.greenpenguin.co.uk

Penguin Random House is committed to a
sustainable future for our business, our readers
and our planet. This book is made from Forest
Stewardship Council® certified paper.

Contents

1. A Chore

The very first contact between Detective Chief Inspector Maigret and the dead man with whom he was to spend several weeks in the most puzzling intimacy was on 27 June 1930 in circumstances that were mundane, difficult and unforgettable all at the same time.

Unforgettable chiefly because for the last week the Police Judiciaire had been getting note after note announcing that the King of Spain would be passing through Paris on that day and reminding them of the precautions to be taken on such an occasion.

It so happened that the commissioner of the Police Judiciaire was in Prague, at a conference on forensics. His deputy had been called home to his villa in Normandy, where one of his children was ill.

Maigret, as the senior inspector, had to take everything on in suffocating heat, with manpower reduced by the holiday season to the bare minimum.

It was also early in the morning of 27 June that the body of a murdered woman, a haberdasher, was found in Rue Picpus.

In short, at nine in the morning all available inspectors had left for Gare du Bois-de-Boulogne, where the Spanish monarch was expected.

Maigret had told his men to open the doors and windows, and in the draughts doors slammed and paper flew off tables.

At a few minutes past nine, a telegram arrived from Nevers:

Émile Gallet, commercial traveller, home address Saint-Fargeau, Seine-et-Marne, murdered night of 25, Hôtel de la Loire, Sancerre. Many curious details. Please inform family for identification of corpse. Send inspector from Paris if possible.

Maigret had no option but to set off in person to Saint-Fargeau, a place thirty-five kilometres from the capital even the name of which had been unknown to him an hour earlier.

He did not know how the trains ran. As he arrived at Gare de Lyon, he was told that a local train was just about to leave. He began to run and was just in time to fling himself into the last carriage. That was quite enough to drench him in sweat, and he spent the rest of the journey getting his breath back and mopping his face, for he was a large, thick-set man.

At Saint-Fargeau he was the only traveller to get out, and he had to wander about on the softened asphalt of the platform for several minutes before he managed to unearth one of the station staff.

'Monsieur Gallet? Right at the end of the central avenue of the housing development. There's a sign outside the house with its name on it, "Les Marguerites". In fact it's almost the only house to be finished so far.'

Maigret took off his jacket, slipped a handkerchief under his bowler hat to protect the back of his neck, because the avenue in question was about 200 metres wide, and you could walk only right down the middle of it, where there was no shade at all.

The sun was an ominous coppery colour, and midges were stinging furiously in advance of the coming storm.

Not a soul in sight to brighten the scene and provide a traveller with any information. The housing development was nothing but a huge forest which must have been part of the grounds of a large manor house. All anyone had done to it yet was to mark out a geometrical network of streets, like the stripes left by a lawnmower, and to lay the cables that would provide the future houses with electric light.

Opposite the railway station, however, there was a square laid out with mosaic-lined fountains. Over a wooden shack was a sign reading 'Sales Office. Plots of Land for Development'. Beside it, there was a map on which the empty streets already bore the names of politicians and generals.

Every fifty metres, Maigret took out his handkerchief to mop his face again, and then put it back over the nape of his neck, which was beginning to sizzle. He saw embryonic buildings here and there, sections of wall that the builders must have abandoned because of the heat. At least two kilometres from the station he found 'Les Marguerites', a house that was faintly English in appearance, with red tiles, complicated architecture and a rustic wall separating the garden from what for a few years yet would still be the forest.

Looking up through the first-floor windows, he saw a bed with a mattress folded in two on top of it, while the sheets and blankets were airing over the window-sill.

He rang the bell. A maidservant about thirty years old with a squint looked at him through a peephole first, and while she was making up her mind to open the door Maigret put his jacket back on.

'I'd like to see Madame Gallet, please.'

'Who shall I say it is?'

But a voice inside the house was already asking her, 'Who is it, Eugénie?'

And Madame Gallet appeared on the steps in person, chin in the air as she waited for the intruder to explain himself.

'You've dropped something,' she said in unfriendly tones, as he took off his hat, forgetting the handkerchief, which now fell to the ground.

He picked it up, mumbling something unintelligible, and introduced himself. 'Detective Chief Inspector Maigret of the Flying Squad. I would like a few words with you, madame.'

'With me?' And she added, turning to the maid, 'What are you waiting about for?'

Maigret knew what he thought about Madame Gallet, at least. She was a woman of around fifty, and there were no two ways about it: she was disagreeable. In spite of the time of day, the heat, the solitude of the house, she was already wearing a mauve silk dress, and not one of her grey hairs ventured out of the rigidity of her set. Her neck, bosom and hands were laden with gold necklaces, brooches and rings that clicked against each other. Unwillingly, she preceded her visitor into the sitting room. As he passed an open door, Maigret saw a white kitchen sparkling with copper and aluminium pans.

'May I start waxing the floor, madame?'

'Of course! Why not?'

The maid disappeared into the dining room next door and could soon be heard spreading wax polish on the floor where she knelt, while an invigorating smell of turpentine spread through the house. There were pieces of embroidery on all the furniture in the sitting room. On the wall hung an enlarged photograph of a tall, thin adolescent boy with jutting knees, dressed for his First Communion.

A smaller photo on the piano showed a man with thick hair, a salt-and-pepper goatee beard, wearing a jacket with poorly cut shoulders. The oval of his face was as long as the boy's. Another detail brought Maigret up short, and it was several moments before he realized that the man's lips, which almost cut his face in half, were abnormally thin.

'Your husband?'

'Yes, my husband! And I am waiting to hear what the police think they are doing here . . .'

During the conversation that followed, Maigret had to keep looking back at the photograph, and that could really be described as his first point of contact with the dead man.

'I'm afraid I have bad news to break, madame . . . your husband is away, isn't he?'

'Well, go on! Out with it . . . has something . . . ?'

'Yes, there has been an accident. Well, not strictly speaking an accident. I must ask you to be brave . . .'

She was standing in front of him, her back very straight, her hand resting on a pedestal table with a reproduction bronze on it. Her face was hard, distrustful, and nothing about her moved except her podgy fingers. What made Maigret think that she had certainly been slim, maybe very slim, for the first half of her life, and had put on weight only with age?

'Your husband was killed in Sancerre on the night of 25 June. I have the painful task of informing you . . .'

The inspector turned to the portrait photo and asked, pointing to the boy dressed for his First Communion, 'You have a son, I believe?'

For a moment Madame Gallet looked as if the straight back that she thought indispensable to her dignity might be about to bend. She said, reluctantly, 'A son, yes,' and then she immediately added, in a triumphant tone, 'You did say Sancerre, didn't you? And this is the 27th. In that case you've made a mistake. Wait a minute . . .'

She went into the dining room, where Maigret could see the maid on all fours. When Madame Gallet came back, she held a postcard out to her visitor.

'This card is from my husband. It's dated the 26th and postmarked Rouen.'

She had some difficulty in suppressing a smile betraying her delight in humiliating a police officer who was bold enough to intrude on her privacy.

'It must be some other Gallet, not that I know anyone of that name.' She was almost on the point of opening the door, and couldn't keep her eyes off it. 'My husband represents the firm of Niel et Cie all over Normandy.'

'I'm afraid, madame, that your relief is unfounded. I must ask you to accompany me to Sancerre. For both your sake and mine . . .'

'But since . . .'

She shook the postcard, which showed the Old Market in Rouen. The door of the dining room was still open, and Maigret could see now the maid's behind and feet, now her head and the hair falling over her face. He heard the sound of the rag, greasy with polish, being wiped over the wooden floor.

'Believe me, I wish with all my heart that there was some mistake. However, the papers found in the dead man's pockets are definitely your husband's.'

'They could have been stolen from him . . .' But despite

herself, a note of anxiety was beginning to creep into her voice. She followed Maigret's eyes as he looked at the smaller portrait and said, 'That photo was taken when he had begun dieting.'

'If you would like to eat lunch first,' suggested the inspector, 'I could come back for you in an hour's time.'

'Certainly not. If you think that . . . that it's necessary . . . Eugénie! My black silk coat, my bag and my gloves.'

Maigret was not interested in this case; it had all the hallmarks of a particularly distasteful investigation. And if he remembered the picture of the man with the goatee beard – who was dieting! – and the boy dressed for his First Communion, it was unintentionally.

Everything he did today felt like a chore. First going back up the central avenue in an increasingly stifling atmosphere, and this time unable to take his jacket off. Then waiting thirty-five minutes at Melun station, where he bought a picnic basket containing sandwiches, fruit and a bottle of Bordeaux.

At 3 p.m. he was sitting opposite Madame Gallet in a first-class compartment, in a train on the main line to Moulins, stopping at Sancerre. The curtains were drawn, the windows lowered, but there was only a very occasional breath of fresh air.

Maigret had taken his pipe out of his pocket; but when he looked at his companion he gave up any idea of smoking in front of her. The train had been going along for a good hour when she asked, in a voice that at last sounded more human, 'How would you explain all this?'

'I can't explain anything yet, madame. I don't know anything. As I told you, the crime was committed on the night of 25 June, at the Hôtel de la Loire. This is the holiday season, and in addition the provincial prosecutors' offices aren't always in a hurry. We weren't told at police headquarters in Paris until this morning ... Was your husband in the habit of sending you postcards?'

'Whenever he was away.'

'He was away a great deal?'

'About three weeks a month. He went to Rouen and stayed at the Hôtel de la Poste ... he's been staying there for twenty years! He based himself there and went out all over Normandy, but he managed to get back to Rouen in the evening as often as possible.'

'You have only the one son?'

'One son, yes! He works in a bank in Paris.'

'Rather than living with you in Saint-Fargeau?'

'It's too far for him to come home every day. He always spends Sundays with us.'

'May I suggest that you have something to eat?'

'No thank you,' she said, in the same tone that she might have used to reply to an impertinent remark. And indeed, he had difficulty in imagining her nibbling a sandwich like the first to arrive at a party, and drinking warm wine from the catering company's oiled paper cup. You could tell that dignity meant a great deal to her. She could never have been pretty, but she had regular features, and if she had not been so expressionless she would not have been without charm, thanks to a certain melancholy in her face which was emphasized by her way of holding her head on one side.

'Why would anyone kill my husband?' she wondered aloud.

'You don't know of any enemies he may have had?'

'No enemies, no friends either! We live very quietly, like everyone who's known a time before all the brutality and vulgarity you find now that the war is over.'

'I see.'

The journey seemed interminable. Several times Maigret went out into the corridor for a few puffs at his pipe. His detachable collar had gone limp owing to the heat and his profuse perspiration. He envied Madame Gallet, who didn't even notice temperatures of 33 or 34 degrees in the shade and stayed in exactly the same position as at the start of the journey, as if for a bus trip, handbag on her knees, head slightly turned to the window.

'How was th . . . that man killed?'

'The telegram doesn't say. I gathered that he was found dead in the morning.'

Madame Gallet jumped, and it took her a moment to get her breath back as she sat with her mouth half open.

'It can't possibly be my husband. Surely that card proves it? I shouldn't even have had to go to all this bother.'

Without knowing just why, Maigret regretted not bringing the photo from the piano, because he was already having trouble reconstructing the top part of the face in his mind. On the other hand, he clearly visualized the over-long mouth, the small, thick beard, the poorly cut shoulders of the jacket.

It was seven in the evening when the train stopped at Tracy-Sancerre station, and they still had to walk a kilometre along the main road and cross the suspension bridge over the River Loire, which did not offer the majestic view of a river but the sight of a great many streams of water running fast between sandbanks the colour of over-ripe wheat. A man in a nankeen suit was fishing on one of these islets. And now the Hôtel de la Loire came into view, its yellow façade running along the bank. The rays of the sun slanted more now, but it was still difficult to breathe the air, thick with so much water vapour.

Madame Gallet was in the lead now, and seeing a man who must be a colleague of his pacing up and down outside the hotel, Maigret disliked the thought that he and his companion looked a perfectly ridiculous couple.

People on holiday, mostly families, wearing pale clothes, were sitting at tables under a glazed roof, with waitresses in aprons and white caps walking around.

Madame Gallet had seen the sign bearing the name of the hotel surrounded by the crests of several clubs. She made straight for the door.

'Police Judiciaire?' asked the man pacing up and down, stopping Maigret.

'Yes, what is it?'

'He's been taken to the town hall. You'd better hurry up – the post-mortem is at eight. You'll be just in time.'

Just in time to get acquainted with the dead man. At that moment, Maigret was still dragging himself about like a man doing a difficult and unattractive task.

Later, he had time to remember the second point of contact at his leisure. It could not be followed by another.

The village was glaring white in the stormy light of that late afternoon. Chickens and geese crossed the main road, and fifty metres away two men in aprons were shoeing a horse.

Opposite the town hall, people were sitting at tables on a café terrace, and from the shade of red and yellow striped awnings rose an atmosphere of cool beer, ice cubes floating in sweet-smelling drinks and newspapers just arrived from Paris.

Three cars were parked in the middle of the square. A nurse was looking for the pharmacy. In the town hall itself, a woman was washing down the grey-tiled corridor.

'Excuse me. The body?'

'Back there! In the school playground. The gentlemen are over there . . . you can come this way.'

She pointed to a door with the word 'Girls' over it; it said 'Boys' above the other wing of the building.

Madame Gallet went ahead with unexpected self-assurance, but all the same Maigret thought she was more likely in some kind of daze.

In the school yard, a doctor in a white coat was smoking a cigarette and walking about like a man expecting something. Sometimes he rubbed his very delicate hands together. Two other people were talking under their breath, near a table with a body stretched out on it under a white sheet.

The inspector tried to slow his companion down, but he had no time to get there first. She was already in the yard, where she stopped in front of the table, held her breath and suddenly raised the sheet over the dead man's face.

She did not cry out. The two men who were talking had turned to her in surprise. The doctor put on rubber gloves, went over to a door and asked, 'Isn't Mademoiselle Angèle back yet?'

While he took off one of his gloves to light another cigarette Madame Gallet stood there motionless, very stiff, and Maigret prepared to go to her aid.

She abruptly turned to him, her face full of hatred, and cried, 'How could this happen? Who dared to . . . ?'

'Come this way, madame . . . it is him, isn't it?'

Her eyes moving fast now, she looked at the two men, the doctor in white, the nurse who was on her way, waddling.

'What do we do now?' she managed to say, her voice hoarse.

And when Maigret, embarrassed, hesitated to reply, she finally flung herself on her husband's body, cast a furious glance of anger and defiance at the yard and everyone in it and shouted, 'I don't want to! I don't want to!'

She had to be forcibly removed and handed over to the concierge, who abandoned her buckets of water. When Maigret returned to the yard the doctor had a surgical knife in his hand and a mask over his face, and the nurse was handing him a frosted glass bottle.

Unintentionally, the inspector kicked a small black silk hat, decorated with a mauve bow and an imitation diamond gemstone.

He did not watch the post-mortem. Dusk was near, and the doctor had announced that he had seven guests coming to dinner at Nevers. The two men were the examining magistrate and the clerk of the court. After shaking the inspector's hand, the magistrate merely said, 'As you can see, the local police have begun their investigations. It's a terribly confused case.'

The body was naked under the sheet laid over it, and the dismal conversation lasted only a few seconds. The corpse was much as Maigret would have imagined from the photo of the living man: long, bony, with a bureaucrat's hollow chest, a pale skin that made his hair look very dark, while the body hair on his chest was reddish.

Only half his face was still intact; the left cheek had been blown away by a gunshot.

His eyes were open, but the mid-grey irises looked even more lifeless than in his photograph.

He was dieting, Madame Gallet had said.

Under his left breast there was a neat, regular wound retaining the shape of a knife-blade.

Behind Maigret, the doctor was dancing on the spot with impatience. 'Do I send my report to you? Where are you staying?'

'At the Hôtel de la Loire.'

The magistrate and his clerk looked elsewhere and said nothing. Maigret, looking for the way out, tried the wrong door and found himself among the benches in one of the school classrooms. It was pleasantly cool in there, and the inspector lingered for a moment in front of some lithographs entitled 'Harvest', 'A Farm in Winter' and 'Market Day in Town'. On a shelf all the measures of weight and volume, made of wood, tin and iron, were arranged in order of size.

The inspector mopped his face. As he left the room again, he met the police inspector from Nevers, who was looking for him.

'Oh, good, there you are! Now I can join my wife in Grenoble. Would you believe it . . . yesterday morning when the phone call came I was about to go on holiday!'

'Have you found anything out?'

'Nothing at all. As you'll see, it's a most improbable case. If you'd like we can dine together, and I'll give you the details, if you can call them details. Nothing was stolen. No one saw or heard anything! And it would be a clever fellow who could say why the man was killed.

There's only one oddity, but I don't suppose it will get us very far. When he stayed at the Hôtel de la Loire, as he did from time to time, he checked in under the name of Monsieur Clément, a man of private means, from Orleans.'

'Let's go and have an aperitif,' suggested Maigret.

He remembered the tempting atmosphere of the terrace. Just now it had looked to him like the refuge he dreamed of. However, when he was sitting in front of an ice-cold beer, he did not feel the satisfaction he had anticipated.

'This is the most disappointing imaginable case,' sighed his companion. 'You just take a look at it! Nothing to give us a lead! And what's more, nothing out of the ordinary, except that the man was murdered . . .'

He went on in this vein for several minutes, without noticing that the inspector was hardly listening.

There are some people whose faces you can't forget even if you merely passed them once in the street. All that Maigret had seen of Émile Gallet was a photograph, half of his face, and his pale body. Again, it was the photo that lingered in his mind. And he was trying to bring it to life, to imagine Monsieur Gallet having a private conversation with his wife, in the dining room at Saint-Fargeau, or leaving the villa to catch his train at the station.

In fits and starts, the top part of the man's face took clearer shape in his mind. Maigret thought he remembered that he had ashen bags under his eyes.

'I'll bet he had liver trouble,' he suddenly said under his breath.

'Well, he didn't die of it, anyway!' said his companion tartly, annoyed. 'Liver trouble doesn't blow off half your face and stab you through the heart!'

The lights of a funfair came on in the middle of the square, where a carousel of wooden horses was being dismantled.

2. A Young Man in Glasses

There were only two or three groups of hotel guests still sitting at their tables. Howls of indignation from children being made to go to bed came from the rooms on the first floor.

From the other side of an open window, a woman's voice asked, 'See that big man, did you? He's a policeman! He'll put you in prison if you're naughty . . .'

Still eating, and letting his eyes wander over the scene before him, Maigret heard a persistent droning sound. It was Inspector Grenier from Nevers, talking for the sheer pleasure of talking.

'Now if only he'd had something stolen from him. Then the case would be child's play. This is Monday . . . the crime was committed on the night of Saturday into Sunday . . . it was a holiday. These days, as well as the travelling showmen, and I distrust them on principle, you see all sorts of people prowling round. You don't know what the countryside's like, inspector! You may well be able to find nastier characters here than among the dregs of Paris . . .'

'The fact is,' said Maigret, interrupting him, 'if it hadn't been for the holiday the crime would have been discovered at once.'

'What do you mean?'

'I mean it was because of the rifle range on the fairground and the firecrackers going off that no one heard the gunshot. Didn't you tell me that Gallet didn't die of the injury to his head?'

'So the doctor says, and the post-mortem will confirm that hypothesis. The man got a bullet in his head, but it seems that he could have lived another two or three hours. Directly after the shot, however, he was stabbed in the heart with a knife, and death was instantaneous. The knife has been found.'

'How about the revolver?'

'We haven't found that.'

'The knife was in the room with him?'

'Within a few centimetres of the body, and there are bruises on Gallet's left wrist. It looks as if, knowing he was wounded, he raised the knife in the air as he made for his attacker, but he was weakened . . . Then the murderer grabbed his wrist, twisted it, and ran the blade through his heart. That's not just my own opinion, the doctor thinks so too.'

'So if it hadn't been for the fair, Gallet wouldn't be dead!'

Maigret was not trying to indulge in ingenious deductions or startle his provincial colleague, but the idea struck him and now he was thinking it through, curious to see where it would lead him.

But for all the noise of the wooden carousel horses, the rifle range and the firecrackers, the detonation would have been heard. People from the hotel would have come running, and might have intervened before the knife went into the victim.

Night had fallen now; all you could see were a few reflections of moonlight on the river and the two lamps at the ends of the bridge. Inside the café, guests were playing billiards.

'A strange story,' concluded Inspector Grenier. 'It's not eleven yet, is it? My train leaves at eleven thirty-two, and it will take me quarter of an hour to get to the station. I was saying that if anything had gone missing . . .'

'What time do the fairground stalls close?'

'Midnight. That's the law!'

'Which means that the crime was committed before midnight, and that in turn means that not everyone in the hotel will have been in bed.'

While both officers pursued their own trains of thought, the conversation went on in desultory fashion.

'Like that false name he gave, Monsieur Clément. The proprietor should have told you . . . he stayed here from time to time. About every six months, I'd say. It must be ten years ago that he first came here. He always used the name of Clément, a man of private means, from Orleans.'

'Did he have a case with him – the kind of thing commercial travellers use for their samples?'

'I didn't see anything like that in his room . . . but the hotel proprietor can tell you. Monsieur Tardivon! Come here a minute, would you? This is Inspector Maigret from Paris, and he'd like to ask you a question. Did Monsieur Clément usually have a commercial traveller's case with him?'

'Containing silverware,' Inspector Maigret added.

'Oh no. He always had a travelling bag for his personal things, because he was very careful about looking after himself. Wait a minute! I didn't see him much in an ordinary jacket. Most of the time he wore a waisted one with tails, either black or dark grey.'

'Thank you.'

Maigret thought about the firm of Niel et Cie, which Monsieur Gallet represented all over Normandy. It specialized in gold and silverware for gifts: rattles, reproduction mugs, silver place settings, fruit baskets, sets of knives, cake slices . . .

He ate the tiny piece of almond cake that a waitress had put in front of him and filled his pipe.

'A little glass of something?' asked Monsieur Tardivon. 'I don't mind if I do.'

Monsieur Tardivon went in search of the bottle himself and then sat down at the table with the two police officers.

'So you'll be in charge of the inquiries, inspector? What a thing, eh? Right at the beginning of the season, too! What would you say if I told you seven guests left this hotel this morning to go to the Commercial Hotel instead! Your very good health, gentlemen! Now, as for this Monsieur Clément . . . I'm used to calling him that, you see . . . and who could have known it wasn't his real name?'

More and more people were leaving the terrace. A waiter was taking the bay trees in wooden containers that stood among the tables and lining them up against the wall. A goods train passed along the opposite bank, and the eyes of the three men automatically followed the reddish light as it moved along the foot of the hill.

Monsieur Tardivon had begun his career as a cook in a big house and still had a certain air of solemnity from those days, a very slightly contrived way of bowing towards the person he was talking to.

'The really extraordinary thing,' he said, cradling his glass of Armagnac in the palm of his hand, 'is that the crime was within a hair's breadth of not being committed at all . . .'

'Yes, the funfair,' Grenier quickly put in, glancing at Maigret.

'I don't know what you mean . . . no, when Monsieur Clément arrived on Saturday morning I gave him the blue room, the one that looks out on what we call the nettle lane. It's the lane over there on the left. We call it that because now it's not used for anything it's been invaded by nettles . . .'

'Why isn't it used for anything?' asked Maigret.

'See that wall just beyond the lane? It's the wall of Monsieur de Saint-Hilaire's villa. Well, here in the country we usually call it the little chateau, to distinguish it from the big one, the old chateau of Sancerre above the hill. You can see its turrets from here, and it has very fine grounds. Well, in the old days, before the Hôtel de la Loire was built, the grounds came up to here, and the grand front entrance with a wrought-iron gate was at the end of the nettle lane. The gate is still there, but no one uses it, because they've made another entrance on the riverbank 500 metres away . . . In short, I gave Monsieur Clément the blue room with windows looking out this way. It's quiet, no one ever goes along the lane because it doesn't lead anywhere. I don't know why, but the afternoon when he came back he asked if I didn't have a room with a view of the yard. But I didn't have another vacancy. There's a big choice in the winter because I get hardly anyone then but the regulars, commercial travellers going round at fixed times, but the summer . . . that's different! Believe it or not, most of my guests come from Paris! There's nothing like the air of the Loire . . . Well, so I told Monsieur Clément that I couldn't oblige him, and I did point out that his room was the best in the hotel. With a view of the yard you get chickens and geese, and water being drawn from the well at all sorts of times. And no matter how much grease we put on it, that chain makes a screeching noise. He didn't persist . . . but if only I *had* had a room with a view of the yard, just think . . . he wouldn't be dead now!'

'Why not?' murmured Maigret.

'Didn't anyone tell you that the shot was fired from at least six metres away? And the room is only five metres wide, so the murderer must have been outside, taking advantage of the fact that the nettle lane is deserted. He couldn't have got into the yard to fire his gun, and besides, people would have heard it. Another little drink, gentlemen? It's on the house, of course.'

'So that makes two!' said the inspector.

'Two what?' asked Grenier.

'Two coincidences. First the fair had to be in full swing, to muffle the sound of the shot. And then all the rooms looking out on the yard had to be occupied . . .' He turned to Monsieur Tardivon, who had just refilled their glasses. 'How many guests do you have here at the moment?'

'Thirty-four, counting the children.'

'And none of them have left since the crime was committed?'

'Yes, I told you. Seven have left: a family from the suburbs of Paris – Saint-Denis, I think. A mechanic of some kind, with his wife, his mother-in-law, his sister-in-law and their kids. Not very well-educated people, incidentally. I can't say I was sorry to see them move to the Commercial. We all have our own kinds of regulars, and here, as everyone will agree, you meet only a nice class of guests . . .'

'How did Monsieur Clément spend his days?'

'I couldn't really say . . . he went for walks. Wait a moment, I had an idea that he has a child somewhere around here . . . a child out of wedlock. That's just an idea, because in spite of yourself you try to work things out. He was very polite, and there was always a sad look about him. I never saw him eating at the table d'hôte – we do have a table d'hôte in winter, but he liked to sit in a corner dining by himself . . .'

Maigret had taken a notebook out of his pocket, an ordinary notebook with a black waxed cover, the kind a laundrywoman would use. He made some notes in pencil.

1. Send telegram to Rouen;
2. Send telegram to Niel et Cie;
3. Look at hotel yard;
4. Find out about Saint-Hilaire property;
5. Take fingerprints from knife;
6. Get list of guests;
7. Mechanic and family at Commercial Hotel;
8. People who left Sancerre on Sunday the 26th;
9. Get the town crier to announce a reward for anyone who met Monsieur Gallet on Saturday the 25th.

His colleague from Nevers, a forced smile on his lips, was following Maigret's every movement with his eyes.

'Well? Have you come up with an idea already?'

'No, nothing of the sort! I have two telegrams to send now, and then I'm going to bed.'

The only people left in the café were the locals finishing their game of billiards. Maigret glanced at the nettle lane, which had once been the central avenue going up to the little chateau and still had two rows of fine oak trees lining it. These days dense vegetation had invaded everything, and there was nothing to be seen at this hour.

Grenier prepared to set off for the station, and Maigret retraced his steps to shake hands and say goodbye.

'Good luck,' said Grenier. 'Between ourselves, this is a brute of a case, don't you agree? Nothing sensational, and no kind of useful lead either. Sooner you than me, to be frank with you.'

Maigret was shown to a room on the first floor, where mosquitoes began to whine around his head. He was in a bad temper. The job ahead was a gloomy prospect, a nondescript case with nothing interesting about it.

And yet once he was in bed, instead of going to sleep he began seeing Gallet's face in his mind's eye, sometimes only one cheek, sometimes only the lower part of the face.

He tossed and turned awkwardly in the damp sheets. He could hear the murmuring of the river as it lapped against the sandbanks.

Every criminal case has a feature of its own, one that you identify sooner or later, and it often provides the key to the mystery.

He thought that the feature of this one was, surely, its sheer mediocrity.

Mediocrity in Saint-Fargeau! A mediocre house! Undistinguished interior decoration, with the portrait photo of the boy about to take his First Communion and the one of his father in an overly tight jacket, both on the piano.

More mediocrity in Sancerre! A low-budget holiday resort! A second-class hotel!

All these details added to the dull, grey atmosphere surrounding the case.

A commercial traveller for the firm of Niel: fake silverware, fake luxury, fake style!

A funfair, and one with a rifle range and firecrackers into the bargain . . .

And then there was the distinction lent to it all by

Madame Gallet, whose hat adorned with paste diamonds had fallen into the dust of the school playground.

It was a relief to Maigret to find out, in the morning, that the widow had taken the first train back to Saint-Fargeau, and the coffin containing the remains of Émile Gallet was on its way back to Les Marguerites in a hired van.

He was in a hurry to get this case over and done with. Everyone else had left: the magistrate, the doctor with his seven guests coming to dinner, and Inspector Grenier.

As a result, Maigret was left alone with some precise tasks to carry out.

First, he must wait for replies to the two telegrams he had sent the previous evening.

Then examine the room where the crime had been committed. Finally, think about all those who *could have* committed the crime and who were therefore suspects.

He did not have to wait long for the reply from Rouen. It came from the police of that city:

Have questioned staff of Hôtel de la Poste. Cashier, Irma Strauss, said a man called Émile Gallet sent her an envelope containing postcards to be forwarded. Received 100 francs a month for her trouble. Has been doing this for five years, and thinks that the cashier before her did the same.

Half an hour later, at ten o'clock, a telegram from the firm of Niel arrived:

Émile Gallet has not worked for our firm since 1912.

This was the moment when the town crier began doing his rounds. Maigret, who had just finished breakfast, was examining the hotel yard (which had nothing in particular about it) when he was told that the road-mender would like a word with him.

'I was on the road to Saint-Thibaut,' he explained, 'when I saw that Monsieur Clément. I knew him, see, because I'd met him a few times, and I knew his jacket. There was a young man just coming down the road from the farm, and they met face to face. I was sort of like a hundred metres from them, but I could see they were arguing . . .'

'And did they walk away from each other at once?'

'Oh no, they like went up the hill at the end of the road. Then the old man came back on his own, and it wasn't 'til half an hour later in the square that I saw the young man again at the Commercial.'

'What did he look like?'

'Tall, thin . . . with a long face and glasses.'

'What was he wearing?'

'Couldn't rightly say. Might've been something grey . . . or black. So do I get the fifty francs?'

Maigret gave him the money and set off for the Commercial Hotel, where he had drunk his aperitif the evening before.

Yes, he was told, the young man had had lunch there on Saturday 25 June, but the waiter who served him was now on holiday at Pouilly, some twenty kilometres away.

'Are you sure he didn't spend the night here?'

'He'd be in our register if he had.'

'And no one remembers him?'

The cashier recollected that someone had asked for pasta without any butter, and she added that it had to be cooked specially for him.

'It was a young man sitting over there, to the left of that pillar. He had an unhealthy complexion.'

It was beginning to get hot, and Maigret no longer felt the same bored indifference as he had early in the morning.

'Did he have a long face? Thin lips?'

'Yes, a kind of a wide mouth with a scornful look to it. He didn't want coffee or a liqueur or anything . . . some guests are like that, you know . . .'

What had made Maigret think of the photograph of the lad dressed for his First Communion?

The inspector was forty-five years old. He had spent half his life in various branches of the police force: Vice Squad, Traffic, Drug Squad, Railway Police, Gambling Squad. It was quite enough to dispel any vaguely mystical ideas and kill faith in intuition stone dead.

But all the same, for almost twenty-four hours he had been haunted by those two portrait photographs, father and son, and also by an ordinary little phrase from Madame Gallet: 'He was on a diet . . .'

It was without any very clear idea in his mind that he made for the post office and a telephone, and asked for the town hall of Saint-Fargeau.

'Hello. Police Judiciaire . . . can you tell me when Monsieur Gallet's funeral is taking place?'

'At eight o'clock tomorrow.'

'In Saint-Fargeau?'

'Here, yes.'

'One more question! Who am I speaking to?'

'The Saint-Fargeau schoolteacher.'

'Do you know Monsieur Gallet junior?'

'Well, I've seen him several times. He came for the papers this morning.'

'What does he look like?'

'How do you mean?'

'Is he tall, thin?'

'Yes . . . yes, rather.'

'Does he wear glasses?'

'Wait a minute. Yes, now I remember. Horn-rimmed glasses.'

'You don't happen to know if he's unwell?'

'How would I know? He's pale, certainly.'

'Thank you very much.'

Ten minutes later, the inspector was back at the Commercial.

'Madame, can you tell me whether your guest at lunch on Saturday wore glasses?'

The cashier searched her memory and finally shook her head. 'Yes . . . well, no, I can't remember. We get so much passing trade in the summer! It was his mouth I noticed most. In fact, I even said to the waiter, that man has a mouth like a toad's . . .'

It took Maigret longer to track the road-mender down, because he was busy drinking his fifty francs away with some friends in a little bistro tucked away behind the church.

'You told me that the man you saw wore glasses.'

'The young one, that's right. Not the old one.'

'What sort of glasses?'

'Well, round, know what I mean? With dark rims . . .'

On getting up that morning, Maigret had been glad to hear that the body had been taken away. And Madame Gallet, the magistrate, the doctor and the local police officers had also left. He hoped that now he could focus on an objective problem at last, and put the strange appearance of the old man with the beard out of his mind.

He took the train for Saint-Fargeau at three in the afternoon.

For a start all he had seen of Émile Gallet was a photograph. Then he had seen half his face.

Now all he would find would be a coffin permanently closed. And yet, as the train moved away, he had the disagreeable feeling that he was running after the dead man.

Back in Sancerre a disappointed Monsieur Tardivon told his regulars as he offered them a glass of Armagnac:

'A man who looked the serious kind . . . a man of our own age! And he heads off without even going into the room! Do you want to see the place *where he died*? Funny thing, that. However, the Nevers police are no better . . . when they took the body away they drew its outline on the floor first, in chalk. Mind you don't touch anything . . . huh! You never know where a thing like this will lead you.'

3. Henry Gallet's Replies

Maigret, who had spent the night at home in the Boulevard Richard-Lenoir, arrived in Saint-Fargeau on the Wednesday a little before eight in the morning. He was already out of the station when he had second thoughts, retraced his steps and asked the clerk in the ticket office, 'Did Monsieur Gallet often travel by train?'

'Father or son?'

'The father.'

'He went away for three weeks every month. He travelled second class to Rouen.'

'What about the son?'

'He arrives from Paris almost every Saturday evening on a third-class return ticket, and goes back by the last train on Sunday . . . Who could ever have foreseen that . . . ! I can still see him opening the fishing season . . .'

'Father or son?'

'The father, for heaven's sake! By the way, the blue skiff you can see among the trees is his. Everyone's going to want to buy that skiff. He made it himself out of best oak, thinking up all sorts of little improvements. It was like the gadgets he made . . .'

Conscientiously, Maigret added this little detail to the still very sketchy idea he had of the dead man. He looked at the skiff, the Seine, tried to imagine the man with the goatee beard sitting perfectly still for hours with a bamboo fishing rod in his hand.

Then he set off for Les Marguerites, noticing that an empty, fairly well-appointed hearse was travelling the same way. There was no one to be seen near the house, except for a man pushing a wheelbarrow, who stopped at the sight of the hearse, no doubt interested to see the funeral procession.

The bell on the gate had been wrapped in a linen cloth, and the front door was draped in black, with the dead man's initials picked out in silver embroidery.

Maigret had not expected so much pomp and ceremony. To the left, in the corridor, there was a tray with a single card on it, one corner turned down, from the Mayor of Saint-Fargeau.

The sitting room where Madame Gallet had received the inspector had been turned into a temporary chapel of rest. Its furniture must have been moved into the dining room. Black hangings covered the walls, and the coffin stood in the middle of the room, surrounded by candles.

It was hard to say why the scene seemed so odd. Perhaps because there were no visitors, and you could guess that there would not be any, although the hearse was already at the door.

That lone visiting card, a fake lithograph! All those silver tears! And two silhouettes, one on each side of the coffin: Madame Gallet on the right in full mourning, a crape veil over her face, a rosary of matt beads in her fingers; Henry Gallet on the left, also entirely in funereal black.

Maigret moved forward in silence, dipped a sprig of box into the holy water and sprinkled the water over the coffin. He felt that mother and son were following him with their eyes, but no one said a word. Then he moved back into a corner, on the alert for sounds from outside and at the same time watching the young man's facial expressions. Sometimes one of the horses drawing the hearse pawed the path with a hoof. The undertakers' men were talking under their breath out in the sunlight, close to the window. In the funereal room, lit only by the candles, young Monsieur Gallet's irregular face looked even more irregular because all the black emphasized the unhealthy pallor of his skin. His hair, separated by a parting, clung close to his scalp. He had a high, bumpy forehead. It was difficult to catch his troubled gaze as he peered short-sightedly through the thick lenses of his horn-rimmed glasses.

Sometimes Madame Gallet dabbed her eyes with her mourning handkerchief. Henry's gaze never focused on anything for long. It slid over things, always avoiding the inspector, who was relieved to hear the steps of the undertaker's men.

A little later, the stretcher bumped into the corridor walls as it was carried in. Madame Gallet uttered a small sob, and her son patted her on the shoulder while still looking elsewhere.

There was a great contrast between the ostentatious splendour of the hearse and the two figures who began to walk after it, preceded by a puzzled master of ceremonies.

It was still as hot as ever. The man with the wheelbarrow made the sign of the cross, and went off along another path, while the funeral procession, taking small steps, went down the avenue, which was wide enough for regiments to march down it.

A small group of locals gathered in the square as the religious ceremony took place, but Maigret went off into the town hall, where he found no one. He had to go and fetch the schoolteacher, whose classroom was next to the town hall, and the children were left to their own devices for a little while.

'All I can tell you,' said the teacher, 'is what's recorded in our registers. Wait, here we are:

'Gallet, Émile Yves Pierre, born Nantes, 1879, married Aurore Préjean in Paris, October 1902 . . . A son, Henry, born in Paris 1906, registered at the town hall of the IXth arrondissement . . .'

'Don't the local people like them?'

'It's just that the Gallets, who had the villa built in 1910 when the forest was sold off in plots, never wanted to see anyone . . . they're very proud. I've been known to spend a whole Sunday fishing in my skiff less than ten metres away from Gallet's. If I needed something he'd let me have it, but I wouldn't get the slightest bit of conversation out of him afterwards . . .'

'How much do you think this lifestyle cost?'

'I can't say exactly, because I don't know what he spent when he was away, but they'll have needed at least 2,000 francs a month just for the upkeep of their household. If you've seen the villa, you'll know that it has every convenience. They send to Corbeil or Melun for almost everything they need . . . and that's another thing that . . .'

But looking out of the window, Maigret saw the funeral procession going round the church and into the graveyard. He thanked the teacher and, once out in the road again, heard the first spadeful of earth falling on the coffin.

He did not let the mourners see him but went a long way round back to the villa and was careful to arrive a little while after the Gallets. The maid opened the door to him and looked at him hesitantly.

'Madame can't . . .' she began.

'Tell Monsieur Henry that I need to talk to him.'

The squinting maidservant left him outside. A few moments later, the figure of the young man appeared in the corridor. He came towards the doorway and asked, looking past Maigret, 'Couldn't you postpone this visit to another day? My mother is absolutely devastated.'

'I have to talk to you today. Please forgive me if I insist.'

Henry half turned, thus implying that the police officer had only to follow him. He hesitated at the doors on the ground floor and finally opened the door to the dining room, where the sitting-room furniture had been stacked so that you could hardly get round it. Maigret saw the portrait photo of Henry as a boy ready for his First Communion, but looked in vain for the photo of Émile Gallet. Henry did not sit down or say anything, but he took off his glasses to clean the lenses with a gesture of annoyance, while his eyelashes fluttered as he adjusted to the bright light.

'I'm sure you know that it is my job to find whoever killed your father.'

'Yes, which is why I'm surprised to see you here, at a time when it would be more proper to leave my mother and me alone!'

And Henry put his glasses back on, pulling up a double cuff that had slipped down over a hand covered with the same reddish hairs as the chest of the dead man in Sancerre. There was not so much as a twitch on his bony and rather horsy face, with its strong features and gloomy expression. He was leaning his elbow on the piano, which had been moved sideways, showing its green baize back.

'I'd like to ask you for some information about both your father and the whole family.'

Henry did not open his mouth or move a muscle but stood in the same place, icy and funereal.

'Please would you tell me where you were on Saturday 25 June, around four in the afternoon?'

'Before that I'd like to ask *you* a question. Am I obliged to see you and reply to you at a time like this?' He spoke in the same neutral voice suggesting boredom, as if every syllable tired him.

'You're at liberty not to answer. However, let me point out that . . .'

'At what point in your inquiries did you find out who I was?'

Maigret did not reply to that, and to tell the truth he was stunned by this unexpected turning of the tables. It was all the more unexpected because it was impossible to detect the least subtlety on the young man's features. Henry let several seconds pass, and the maid could be heard downstairs replying to a summons from the first floor. 'Just coming, madame!'

'Well?'

'Since you know it already, I was there.'

'In Sancerre?'

Henry still did not move a muscle.

'And you were having a discussion with your father on the lane leading to the old chateau.' Maigret was the more nervous of the two of them, since he felt that his remarks were getting nowhere. His voice sounded flat, there was no echo of response to his suspicions. But the most unnerving thing about it was Henry Gallet's silence; he was not trying to explain himself, just waiting.

'Can you tell me what you were doing in Sancerre?'

'Going to visit my mistress, Éléonore Boursang, who is on holiday and staying at the Pension Germain on the road from Sancerre to Saint-Thibaut.' He almost imperceptibly raised his eyebrows, which were as thick as Émile Gallet's.

'You didn't know your father was in Sancerre?'

'If I'd known I'd have avoided meeting him.' Still the minimum of explanation, forcing the inspector to repeat his questions.

'Did your parents know you were having an affair?'

'My father suspected. He was against it.'

'What was the subject of your conversation?'

'Are you making inquiries about the murderer or his victim?' asked the young man deliberately slowly.

'I'll know who the murderer was when I know enough about the victim. Was your father angry with you?'

'Sorry . . . I was the angry one – I was angry with him for spying on me.'

'And then?'

'Then nothing! He treated me like a disrespectful son. How kind of you to remind me of that today.'

To his relief, Maigret heard footsteps on the stairs. Madame Gallet appeared, as dignified as ever, her neck adorned by a triple necklace of heavy dark stones.

'What is going on?' she asked, looking at Maigret and her son in turn. 'Why didn't you call me, Henry?'

There was a knock, and the maid came in. 'The upholsterers have come to take the draperies away.'

'Keep an eye on them,' said Madame Gallet.

'I came in search of information which I consider indispensable for finding out who the murderer is,' said Maigret, in a voice that was becoming rather too dry. 'I recognize that this is not the ideal moment, as your son has pointed out. But every hour that passes will make it more difficult to arrest the man who killed your husband.' His eyes moved to Henry, who was still looking gloomy.

'When you married Émile Gallet, madame, did you have a fortune of your own?'

She stiffened slightly, and then, with a tremor of pride in her voice, announced, 'I am the daughter of Auguste Préjean!'

'Forgive me, but I . . .'

'The former secretary to the last Bourbon prince and editor of the legitimist journal *Le Soleil*. My father spent all he had on publishing that journal, which went on fighting the good fight.'

'Do you still have any family?'

'I must have, but I haven't seen them since my marriage.'

'You were advised against marrying Monsieur Gallet?'

'What I've just told you ought to help you to understand. All my family are royalists. All my uncles occupied prominent positions, and some of them still do. They did not like it when I married a commercial traveller.'

'Then you were penniless on your father's death?'

'My father died a year after my marriage. At the time when we married my husband had some 30,000 francs . . .'

'What about his family?'

'I never knew them. He avoided mentioning them . . . all I know is that he had an unhappy childhood and that he spent several years in Indochina.'

There was the suggestion of a scornful smile on her son's lips.

'I am asking you these questions, madame, because for

one thing I have just heard that your husband has not in fact worked for the firm of Niel for the last eighteen years.'

She looked at the inspector, and then Henry, and protested emphatically, 'Monsieur . . .'

'I have the information from Monsieur Niel himself.'

'Perhaps, monsieur, it would be better . . .' began the young man, moving towards Maigret.

'No, Henry! I want to prove that what he says is false, it's an odious lie! Come with me, inspector. Come along, follow me!'

And, showing some liveliness for the first time, she made for the corridor, where she came up against the piles of black draperies being rolled up by the upholsterers. She took the inspector up to the first floor, through a bedroom with polished walnut furniture, where Émile Gallet's straw hat still hung on a hook, as well as a cotton drill outfit that he must have worn for fishing. Next came a small room furnished as a study.

'Look at that! Here are his samples. And those place settings, for instance, in that dreadful Art Deco style, you wouldn't say they were eighteen years old, would you? Here's the book of orders that my husband wrote up at the end of every month. Here are some letters that he received regularly, on the Niel letterhead . . .'

Maigret was paying very little attention to this. He felt sure that he would have to come back to this room and just now he preferred to let its atmosphere sink in. He tried to imagine Émile Gallet sitting here in the swivel chair at his desk. On the desk itself there was a white metal inkwell and a glass globe acting as a paperweight. Through the window you could see the central avenue and the red roof of another uninhabited villa.

The letters on the Niel letterhead were typed in an almost regular typeface:

Dear sir,

We have received your letter of the 15th inst., as well as the statement of orders for January. We shall expect you at the end of the month to settle our account, as usual, and we will then give you some information about the expansion of your sphere of activity.

With good wishes,

Signed: Jean Niel

Maigret picked up some of the letters and put them into his wallet.

'So what do you think now?' asked Madame Gallet, with a touch of defiance.

'What's that?'

'Oh, nothing . . . my husband liked to do things with his hands. Here's an old watch that he took apart . . . and out in the shed there are all kinds of things that he made himself, including fishing gear. Every month he had a full week to spend here, and writing up his accounts and so forth took him only an hour or two in the morning . . .'

Maigret was opening drawers at random. He saw a large pink file in one of them, with the word 'Soleil' written on it.

'Some of my father's papers,' explained Madame Gallet. 'I don't know why we kept them. There are copies of all the numbers of the journal in that cupboard, right up to the last one. My father sold his bonds to bring that out.'

'May I take this file away?'

She turned to the door as if to consult her son, but

Henry had not followed them. 'But what can it possibly tell you? It's a kind of relic . . . Still, if you think . . . . Oh, but listen, inspector, it surely must be impossible that Monsieur Niel said . . . I mean, it's like those postcards! I had another one yesterday, and in his writing, I'm sure of it. Sent from Rouen, like the other card. Read it! *All going well. Will be home on Thursday* . . .' Once again some emotion broke through, but with difficulty. 'I shall almost be expecting him. Thursday is tomorrow.' And she suddenly burst into a fit of tears, but an extraordinarily brief one, just two or three hiccups. She raised her black-bordered handkerchief to her mouth and said in a muted voice, 'Well, let's not stay here.'

They had to go through the bedroom again with its walnut furniture – ordinary but of good quality: a wardrobe with a full-length mirror on it, two bedside tables and an imitation Persian carpet.

Down in the ground-floor corridor, Henry was watching the upholsterers loading the draperies into a van without seeming to see them. He did not even turn his head when Maigret and his mother descended the polished staircase, causing the stairs to creak.

There was an untidy look to the house. The maid came into the sitting room, carrying a litre of red wine and glasses. Two men in overalls were dragging the piano back into it.

'Won't do us any harm!' one of the men was saying indifferently.

Maigret had an impression that he had never had before, and it unnerved him. It seemed to him that the whole truth was here, scattered round him, and everything he saw had its meaning. But to understand it, he would have had to see it clearly, not through a sort of fog that distorted the view. And the fog persisted, created by this woman who resisted her emotions, by Henry whose long face was as impregnable as a safe, by the black draperies now on their way out, in fact by everything and most of all by Maigret's own discomfort, out of place as he was in this house.

He felt ashamed of the pink file that he was taking away like a thief, and he would have had difficulty in explaining why it might come in useful. He would have liked to stay upstairs for some time, alone in the dead man's study, and wander round the shed where Émile Gallet worked on perfecting his fishing equipment.

There was a moment of wavering, with everyone coming and going in the corridor at once. It was lunchtime, and it was obvious that the Gallets were only waiting for the police officer to leave. A smell of fried onions came from the kitchen. The maid was as distraught as the others. All anyone could do was watch the upholsterers restoring the sitting room to its usual state. One of them found the photo of Gallet underneath a tray of liqueurs.

'May I take that with me?' Maigret intervened, turning to the widow. 'I may need it.'

He sensed that Henry's eyes were following him with more scorn than ever.

'If you must . . . I don't have many photographs of him.'

'I promise to let you have it back.'

He could not bring himself to leave. At the moment when the workmen were unceremoniously carrying in an enormous fake Sèvres vase, Madame Gallet hurried forwards.

'Careful! You're going to collide with the mantelpiece.'

And the same mixture of grief and the grotesque, the dramatic and the petty, was still weighing down on Maigret's shoulders in this desolate house, where he felt as if he could see Émile Gallet, whom he had not known alive, wandering in silence, his eyes ashen with his liver trouble, his chest hollow, wearing his poorly cut jacket.

He had slipped the portrait photo into the pink file. He hesitated.

'Please forgive me again, madame . . . I'm leaving, but I'd be glad if your son would come a little way with me.'

Madame Gallet looked at Henry with an anxiety that she could not repress. For all her dignified manner, her measured gestures, her triple necklace of black stones, she too must be feeling *something* in the air.

But the young man himself, indifferent to anything of the kind, went to collect his hat with its crape hatband from a hook.

Their departure seemed more like an escape. The file was heavy. It was only a cardboard folder, and the papers threatened to fall out.

'Would you like some newspaper to wrap that in?' asked Madame Gallet.

But Maigret was already out of the house, and the maid was making for the dining room with a tablecloth and some knives. Henry was walking towards the station, tall and silent, his expression inscrutable.

When the two men were 300 metres away from the house, and the upholsterers were starting the engine of their van, the inspector said, 'I only want to ask you for two things: first Éléonore Boursang's address in Paris, and second your own, and the address of the bank where you work.'

He found a pencil in his pocket and wrote on the pink cover of the file he was holding:

Éléonore Boursang, 27 Rue de Turenne. Banque Sovrinos, 117 Boulevard Beaumarchais. Henry Gallet, Hôtel Belle-vue, 19 Rue de la Roquette.

'Is that all?' asked the young man.

'Thank you, yes.'

'In that case I hope you'll be putting your mind to the murderer now.'

He did not try to judge the effect of this remark, but touched the brim of his hat and set off back up the central avenue.

The van passed Maigret just before he reached the station.

The last fact he picked up that day was by sheer chance. Maigret arrived at the station an hour before the train was due in and found himself alone in the deserted waiting room, in the middle of a swarm of flies. Then he saw a postman with the purple neck of an apoplectic arrive on a bicycle and put his bags down on the table for luggage.

'Do you call at Les Marguerites?' asked the inspector.

The postman, who had not noticed him, swung round. 'What did you say?'

'Police! Do you get a lot of mail to be delivered to Monsieur Gallet?'

'A lot, no. Letters from the firm the poor gentleman worked for. They always came on a certain day. And then there were newspapers . . .'

'What newspapers?'

'Provincial papers, mostly from the Berry and Cher regions. And magazines: *Country Lifestyles*, *Hunting and Fishing*, *Country Homes* . . .'

The inspector noticed that the postman was avoiding his eyes.

'Is there a poste restante office in Saint-Fargeau?'

'How do you mean?'

'Didn't Monsieur Gallet get any other letters?'

The postman suddenly seemed flustered. 'Well, seeing as you know, and seeing as he's dead,' he stammered. 'And anyway it's not like I was even breaking the rules . . . he just asked me not to put some letters into the box but keep them until he was back, when he went away . . .'

'What letters?'

'Oh, not many . . . hardly one every two or three months. Blue envelopes, the cheap sort, with the address typed.'

'They didn't have the sender's address on them?'

'Not the address, no. But I couldn't go wrong because it said on the back, and that was typed too, *From: Monsieur Jacob.* Did I do wrong?'

'Where did these letters come from?'

'Paris.'

'I suppose you didn't notice the arrondissement?'

'I did look . . . but it changed every time.'

'When did the last one arrive?'

'Let's see . . . today is the 29th, right? Wednesday. Well, it was Thursday evening, but I didn't see Monsieur Gallet until Friday morning, when he was going fishing . . .'

'So he went fishing?'

'No, he went home after he gave me five francs, same as usual. I came over all funny when I heard he'd been killed . . . do you think that letter . . . ?'

'Did he leave that same day?'

'Yes . . . hey, is it the train from Melun you're waiting

for? They just rang the bell at the level crossing . . . Will you have to mention this to anyone?'

Maigret had no time to do anything but run to the platform and jump into the only first-class carriage.

4. The Crook among the Legitimists

Arriving for the second time at the Hôtel de la Loire, Maigret responded without warmth to Monsieur Tardivon, who received him with a confidential air, took him to his room and showed him some large yellow envelopes that had arrived for him. They contained the coroner's report and the reports of the gendarmerie and the Nevers municipal police. The Rouen police had sent further information about the cashier Irma Strauss.

'And that's not all!' said the hotel manager exultantly. 'The sergeant from the gendarmerie came to see you. He wants you to phone him as soon as you arrive. And then there's a woman who's already turned up three times, no doubt because of the town crier and his sales pitch.'

'What woman?'

'Mother Canut, the wife of the gardener opposite. I told you about the little chateau, remember?'

'Didn't she say anything, then?'

'She's not that stupid! Since there's a reward on offer she's not about to give anything away, but for all that she may know something.'

Maigret had put the pink file on the table along with the photograph of Gallet.

'Ask someone to find the woman and get me the gendarmerie on the phone.'

A little later he was speaking to the sergeant, who told

him that, according to instructions, he had picked up all the vagrants in the neighbourhood and was holding them at Maigret's disposal.

'Anyone interesting among them?'

'They're vagrants,' was all the sergeant said to that.

Maigret stayed alone in his room for three or four minutes, facing a pile of paperwork. And there was more of it to come! He had sent a telegram to Paris asking for information about Henry Gallet and his mistress, and just in case he had alerted Orleans to find out if there was a Monsieur Clément in that city.

Finally, he hadn't had time yet to look at the room where the crime was committed, or the clothing worn by the dead man, which had been placed in that room after the post-mortem.

At first the case had looked like nothing to speak of. A man who did not seem out of the ordinary had been killed by someone unknown in a hotel room. But each new item of information complicated the problem instead of simplifying it.

'Do I get her to come in and see you, inspector?' called a voice in the yard. 'I've got Mother Canut here.'

A strong, dignified old lady, who had probably cleaned herself up more thoroughly than usual for the occasion, came in, immediately looking for Maigret with the wary glance of a countrywoman.

'Do you have something to tell me?' he asked. 'About Monsieur Clément?'

'It's about the gent who died and got his picture in the paper. You're handing out fifty francs, right?'

'Yes, if you saw him on Saturday 25 June.'

'Suppose I saw him twice?'

'Well, maybe you'll get a hundred! Come on, out with it!'

'First you've got to promise not to say a word to my old man. It's not so much that he likes to be the boss as on account of the hundred francs. All the same, I'd not like Monsieur Tiburce to know I been talking, because it was with him I saw the gent who got killed. First time was in the morning, about eleven, when they were walking in the grounds.'

'Are you sure you recognized him?'

'Sure as I'd recognize you! There aren't so many look like him. Well, they were chatting for maybe an hour. Then I saw them through the sitting-room window in the afternoon, and it looked like they were arguing.'

'What time was that?'

'It had just struck five . . . so that makes twice, right?'

Her eyes were fixed on Maigret's hand as he took a hundred-franc note out of his wallet, and she sighed as if she was sorry she hadn't stuck close to Monsieur Clément's trail all that Saturday.

'And could be I saw him a third time,' she said hesitantly, 'But I s'pose that doesn't count. A few minutes later I saw Monsieur Tiburce taking him back to the gate.'

'You're right, it doesn't count,' agreed Maigret, impelling her towards the door.

He lit a pipe, put his hat on and stopped opposite Monsieur Tardivon in the café. 'Has Monsieur de Saint-Hilaire lived in the little chateau for long?'

'About twenty years.'

'What kind of man is he?'

'Very pleasant fellow! A little, fat man, cheerful, straightforward. When I have guests in summer we hardly see him, because, well, they're not his class. But he often drops in here in the hunting season.'

'Does he have any family?'

'He's a widower. We almost always call him Monsieur Tiburce, because that's not a common first name. He owns all the vines you can see on the slope there. He tends them himself, goes to live it up in Paris now and then and comes back to get his hobnailed boots. What did Mother Canut have to tell you?'

'Do you think Monsieur Tiburce is at home now?'

'Could be. I didn't see his car pass this morning.'

Maigret went to the barred gate and rang the bell, noticing that as the Loire described a bend just outside the hotel, and the villa was the last property in the area, you could go in and out of it at any time without being seen.

Beyond the gate, the wall surrounding the vineyard went on for another three or four hundred metres, and after that there was nothing but undergrowth.

A man with a drooping moustache, wearing a gardener's apron, came to open the gate, and the inspector concluded, from the strong smell of alcohol about him, that he was probably Madame Canut's husband.

'Is your master here?'

At the same moment, Maigret caught sight of a man in shirtsleeves inspecting a mechanical sprinkler. The gardener's glance told him that this was indeed Tiburce de Saint-Hilaire, and moreover, abandoning the device, he turned to the visitor and waited.

Then, as Canut looked awkward, to say the least of it, he finally picked up the jacket that he had left on the grass and came over.

'Is it me you want to see?'

'Detective Chief Inspector Maigret of the Police Judiciaire. Would you be kind enough to give me a moment of your time?'

'That crime again, is it?' The owner of the property jerked his chin at the Hotel de la Loire. 'What can I do for you? Come this way. I won't invite you into the drawing room, because the sun's been beating on the walls all day. We'll be more comfortable under that arbour. Baptiste! Glasses and a bottle of the sparkling wine . . . the row at the back.'

He was just as the hotelier had described him, small and stout, red-faced, with short hands not very well cared for, wearing an off-the-peg khaki hunting and fishing outfit.

'Did you know Monsieur Clément?' asked Maigret, sitting down on one of the wrought-iron chairs.

'According to the newspaper that wasn't his real name, he was called . . . what was it? . . . Grelet? Gellet?'

'Gallet, yes. It doesn't matter. Were you in business with him?'

At that moment, Maigret could have sworn that the other man was not entirely at his ease. Furthermore, Saint-Hilaire felt a need to lean forwards out of the arbour, murmuring, 'That fool Baptiste is perfectly capable of bringing us the demi-sec, and I'm sure you'd rather have the sec, like me. It's our own wine, made by the champenoise method . . . Now, about this Monsieur Clément – might as well go on calling him that – what shall I say? It would be exaggerating to say I was in business with him! But it wouldn't be exactly true to say I'd never seen him either . . .'

As he was talking, Maigret thought of another interrogation, the questions he had asked Henry Gallet. The two men had entirely different attitudes. The murder victim's son did nothing to appear likeable, and he didn't care about the oddity of his attitude either. He waited for questions with a suspicious air, took his time and weighed up his words.

Tiburce talked away with animation, smiled, gestured with his hands, paced up and down, appeared extremely friendly – and yet there was the same latent anxiety in each of them: perhaps the fear of being unable to hide something.

'Well, you know how it is. We country landowners come into contact with all sorts. And I'm not just talking about vagrants, commercial travellers, peripatetic salesmen. Now, to return to this Monsieur Clément . . . Ah, here comes the wine! That's fine, Baptiste. Right, you can be off now. I'll come and look at that sprinkler soon. Whatever you do don't touch it.'

As he spoke, he slowly removed the cork and filled the glasses without spilling a drop.

'So to cut a long story short, he came here once, it's some time ago now. I expect you know that the Saint-Hilaires are a very old family, and at the moment I'm the last offshoot of the family tree. In fact it's a miracle that I'm not a clerk in some office in Paris or further afield. If I hadn't inherited money from a cousin who made his fortune in Asia . . . but never mind, I was going to tell you that my name features in all the yearbooks of the aristocracy. My father, some forty years ago, was noted for his legitimist opinions . . . but so far as I myself am concerned, well, you know!'

He smiled, drank his sparkling wine, clicking his tongue in a distinctly democratic way and waited for Maigret to empty his own glass before refilling it.

'So this Monsieur Clément, whom I don't know from Adam or Eve, came looking for me, got me to read his references from Royal Highnesses in France and elsewhere and then gave me to understand that he was, so to speak, the official representative of the legitimist movement in France. I let him go on talking, and he took his chance to get what he wanted: he was asking me for 2,000 francs for the propaganda fund. And when I said no, he carried on about – oh, some ancient family or other reduced to penury, and a subscription that had been opened for it . . . We began at 2,000 francs, and haggled the sum down to a hundred. In the end I gave him fifty.'

'How long ago was this?'

'Oh, several months. I can't say exactly. It was in the hunting season. The beaters were at work in the grounds of one of the local chateaux here almost every day. I heard about that fellow everywhere and I felt sure he was a specialist in that kind of swindle. But I wasn't about to sue him over fifty francs, was I? To your very good health! Only the other day he had the nerve to come back . . . that's all I know!'

'What day was it?'

'Erm . . . at the weekend.'

'On Saturday, yes. In fact he called twice, if I remember correctly . . .'

'You're brilliant, inspector! Yes, you're right, twice. I refused to see him in the morning. But he buttonholed me in the grounds that afternoon.'

'He was after money?'

'You bet he was, but I'd be hard put to it to say what for. However, he was still on about the restoration of the monarchy. Come on, drink up! It's not worth leaving any in the bottle. Good lord . . . you don't think he committed suicide, do you? He must have been at the end of his tether . . .'

'The shot was fired from seven metres away, and the revolver hasn't been found.'

'In that case, then he didn't. What do you think of it? A vagrant who happened to be passing and . . . ?'

'That's difficult to accept. The windows of the room look out on a lane that leads only to your property.'

'By a disused entrance,' objected Monsieur de Saint-Hilaire. 'It's many years since the gate to the nettle lane was last opened, and I'd be hard put to it to say where the key is . . . How about getting another bottle brought out?'

'No, thank you . . . I don't suppose you heard anything?'

'What kind of thing?'

'The gun being fired on Saturday evening.'

'No, nothing like that. I go to bed early. I didn't hear about the crime until the next morning, when my man-servant told me.'

'And you didn't think of mentioning Monsieur Clément's visit to the police?'

'Good heavens, no . . .' He tried to laugh, covering up for his uneasiness. 'I told myself the poor devil had been punished enough anyway. When you have a name like mine, you don't much like seeing it in the papers anywhere but the society column.'

Maigret still had the same vague and annoying sensation, coming back again and again like a musical chorus: the sensation that everything touching on the death of

Émile Gallet creaked, sounded out of tune and wrong, from the dead man himself to his son's voice, and Tiburce de Saint-Hilaire's laughter.

'You're staying at old Tardivon's place, aren't you? Did you know he used to be a cook at the chateau? He's made a packet since then. Are you sure you won't have another little glass? . . . That fool of a gardener has done something or other to the mechanical sprinkler, and I was just trying to put it right when you turned up . . . out here in the country we have to do everything for ourselves. Well, if you're here for a few days, inspector, come and have a chat with me in the evening now and then. Life in the hotel must be tedious with all those tourists . . .'

At the gate, he took the hand that Maigret had not offered him and shook it with excessive cordiality.

Walking along the side of the Loire, Maigret made a mental note of two points. First, Tiburce de Saint-Hilaire, who must know about the town crier's announcement and thus the importance that the police ascribed to what Monsieur Clément did on the Saturday, had expected to be interrogated and had not in fact said anything until he realized that his interrogator was up to date with the facts already.

Second, he had lied at least once. He had said that on Saturday morning he had refused to see the visitor, who then *buttonholed him in the grounds*.

However, it was the morning when the two men went walking in the grounds. And in the afternoon they had certainly been engaged in conversation *in the drawing room of the villa*.

So the rest of it could also be untrue, the inspector concluded. He was just reaching the nettle lane. On one side of him was the whitewashed wall enclosing Saint-Hilaire's grounds. On the other rose a single-storey building, part of the Hôtel de la Loire. The ground here was overgrown with long grass, brambles and dead nettles, and the wasps were revelling in it all. The oak trees cast a comfortable shade on the avenue, which ended at an old, beautifully worked gate.

Maigret felt curious enough to go up to this gate, which, according to the owner of the property, had not been opened for years and had lost its key. As soon as he looked at the lock, covered with a thick layer of rust, he noticed that in some places that rust had recently been chipped away. This was better! He took out a magnifying glass and saw, without a shadow of doubt, that a key had left scratch marks as it went into the complicated wards of the lock.

I'll get that photographed tomorrow, he thought, making a mental note.

He retraced his steps, head bent, rearranging the picture he had of Monsieur Gallet in his mind's eye, bringing it to light, so to speak. But instead of filling out and becoming more comprehensible, was it not more evasive than ever? The face of the man in the tight-fitting jacket was blurred to the point of having nothing human about it.

Instead of the portrait photo, the only tangible and theoretically complete picture of the murder victim that Maigret had, he saw fleeting images which ought to have made up nothing but one and the same man, but refused to be superimposed into a single whole.

Once again the inspector saw the half of his face, the thin and hairy chest, as he had seen it in the school playground while the doctor danced up and down with impatience behind his back. He also called up images of the blue skiff that Émile Gallet had made in Saint-Fargeau, and the perfectly fashioned fishing tackle, Madame Gallet in mauve silk and then in full mourning, the quintessence of the discreet and formal middle class.

He thought of the wardrobe with the full-length mirror. Gallet must have stood in front of it as he put on his jacket . . . And all that correspondence on the letterheads of the firm that he didn't work for any longer. The monthly statements that he drew up carefully, eighteen years after giving up his job as a commercial traveller!

Those goblets and cake slices *that he had to buy himself*!

Wait a minute, his case of samples hasn't been found yet, thought Maigret in passing. He must have left it somewhere . . .

He had automatically stopped a few metres from the window through which the murderer had aimed at his victim. However, he was not even looking at the window. He was feeling slightly feverish because, at certain moments, he had the impression that with a bit of effort he would be able to reunite all the aspects of Émile Gallet into a single image.

But then he thought of Henry again, both as he knew him, stiffly upright and disdainful, and as a boy with an asymmetrical face ready for his First Communion.

This case, described by Inspector Grenier of Nevers as 'an annoying little case', and one that Maigret had tackled reluctantly, was visibly growing larger as the dead man was transformed to the point of becoming a truly outlandish figure.

Ten times, Maigret brushed aside a wasp hovering close to his head with a noise like a miniature aeroplane.

'Eighteen years!' he said under his breath.

Eighteen years of forged letters signed Niel, of post-cards sent on from Rouen, and all the time he was living his ordinary little life at Saint-Fargeau, without luxuries, without any emotional complications!

The inspector knew the mentality of malefactors, criminals and crooks. He knew that you always find some kind of passion at the root of it.

And that was exactly what he was looking for in the bearded face, the leaden eyelids, the excessively wide mouth.

He made perfectly constructed fishing tackle, and he took old watches apart!

At this point Maigret rebelled.

You don't tell lies for eighteen years just for that, he thought. You don't tie yourself to a double life that is so difficult to organize!

That wasn't the most disturbing part of it. There are difficult situations in which you can manage to live for several months, even several years. But eighteen years! Gallet had grown old! Madame Gallet had put on weight and assumed an air of too much dignity! Henry had grown up . . . he had taken his First Communion, passed his school-leaving exams, come of age, gone to live in Paris, found a mistress . . .

And Émile Gallet went on sending himself letters from the firm of Niel, wrote postcards addressed to his wife in advance, patiently copied out fake lists of orders!

He was on a diet . . .

Maigret could still hear Madame Gallet's voice. He was so deep in his thoughts – thoughts that made his pulse beat faster – that he had let his pipe go out.

Eighteen years without being detected!

It was so unlikely. The inspector, who knew the business

of crime, was better aware of that than anyone! But for the murder, Gallet would have died peacefully in his bed, after leaving all his papers in order. And Monsieur Niel would have been astonished to get an announcement of his death.

It was so extraordinary that the picture the inspector was constructing for himself made him feel an indefinable anxiety, as if it evoked certain phenomena that shake our sense of reality. So it was pure chance that, as he looked up, the inspector saw a darker mark on the white wall round the property, opposite the room that was the scene of the crime.

He went over and saw that the mark was a space between two stones that had recently been enlarged and scuffed by the toe of a shoe. There was a similar mark a little higher up, but less visible. Someone had climbed up the wall, using a branch that hung down to help him . . .

At the very moment when he was about to reconstruct the climb, the inspector swung round. He had the impression that there was an unexpected presence at the end of the road, near the Loire.

He was just in time to see a feminine figure, tall and quite strong, with blonde hair and the regular, clear-cut profile of a Greek statue. The young woman had begun walking on when Maigret turned round, which suggested that she had previously been watching him.

A name sprang to the detective's mind of its own accord: Éléonore Boursang! Up to this point he had not tried to imagine Henry Gallet's mistress. Yet he was suddenly as good as certain that this was the lady.

He quickened his pace and reached the embankment just as she was turning the corner of the main road.

'Back in a minute!' he told the hotelier, who tried to stop him as he was passing.

He ran for a little way while he was out of the fugitive's sight, to reduce the distance between them. Not only did the woman's figure suit the name of Éléonore Boursang, she was exactly the woman that a man like Henry would have chosen.

But on arriving at the crossroads himself, Maigret was annoyed. She had disappeared. He looked into the dimly lit window of a small grocery store and then into the forge next to it.

But it did not matter much, since he knew where to find her.

5. The Thrifty Lovers

The sergeant from the gendarmerie must have formed a seductive idea that morning of the kind of life led by a police officer from Paris. He himself had been up at four in the morning and had already cycled some thirty kilometres, first in the early-morning cold, then in increasingly hot sunlight, when he reached the Hôtel de la Loire for the periodic check carried out on the register of its guests.

It was now 10 a.m. Most of the guests were walking beside the water or bathing in the river. Two horse dealers were talking on the terrace, and the hotelier, a napkin in his hand, was making sure that the tables and the bay trees in their containers were lined up properly.

'Aren't you going to say good morning to the inspector?' asked Monsieur Tardivon, and then, lowering his voice to a confidential tone, 'He's in the room that was the scene of the crime at this very moment. He's had all kinds of papers sent to him from Paris, and big photographs too . . .'

It worked; a little later the sergeant knocked on the door and said, apologetically, 'It was Monsieur Tardivon, inspector. When he told me you were examining the scene I was tempted . . . I know you have special methods in Paris . . . if I'm not in the way I'd really like to learn from seeing how you do it.'

He was an amiable man whose round, pink face showed an ingenuous wish to please, and he made himself as small as possible, not entirely easy in view of his hobnailed boots and his gaiters. He couldn't decide where to put his képi.

The window was wide open, the morning sun fell right on the nettle lane so that against the light the room was almost dark. And Maigret, in his shirtsleeves, pipe between his teeth, detachable collar unbuttoned, tie loose, gave an impression of well-being that was bound to strike the local policeman.

'Sit down, do, by all means. But there's nothing interesting to see, you know.'

'Oh, you're too modest, inspector.'

It was so naive that Maigret turned his head to hide a smile. He had brought everything to do with the case into the room with him. After making sure that the table, covered with an Indian tablecloth that had a reddish leaf pattern, could tell him nothing, he had spread out all his files on it, from the medical examiner's report to photos of the scene and the victim sent to him from Criminal Records that very morning. Finally, giving way to a feeling that was superstitious rather than scientific, he had put the picture of Émile Gallet on the black marble mantelpiece, which had a copper candlestick on it by way of an ornament.

There was no carpet on the varnished oak boards of the floor, on which the first officers to come on the scene had drawn the outline of the body they found there in chalk.

In all the greenery outside the window there was a confused murmuring made up of birdsong, rustling leaves, the buzzing of flies and the distant clucking of chickens on the lane, all of it punctuated by the rhythmic blows of the hammer on the anvil in the forge. Confused voices sometimes came up from the terrace, or the sound of a cart crossing the suspension bridge.

'Well, you're not short of documents! I'd never have thought . . .'

But the inspector wasn't listening. Calmly, taking little puffs at his pipe, he put a pair of black trousers on the floor where the corpse's legs had lain. The fabric was such a fine weave that, after having been worn for some ten years, judging by their shininess, they could surely have been worn for another ten.

Maigret also laid out a percale shirt and, in its usual place, a starched shirt-front. However, there was no shape to this collection, and it was only when he put a pair of elastic-sided shoes at the ends of the trouser legs that it became both absurd and touching.

In fact it did not look like a body, it was more of a caricature, and it was so unexpected that the sergeant glanced at his companion and uttered an embarrassed little laugh.

Maigret did not laugh. Heavy and bent on his task, he was walking up and down slowly, conscientiously. He examined the jacket and put it back in the travelling bag, after making sure that there was no hole in the fabric where the blade of the knife had gone in. The waistcoat, which was torn level with its left pocket, took its place on the shirt-front.

'That's how he was dressed,' he said under his breath.

He consulted one of the police photographs and adjusted his handiwork by giving his imaginary dummy a very high detachable celluloid collar and a black satin tie.

'See that, sergeant? He dined at eight on Saturday – he had some pasta because he was on a diet. Then he read the paper and drank mineral water, as usual. A little while after 10 p.m. he entered this room and took off his jacket, keeping on his shoes and his detachable collar.'

In fact Maigret was talking not so much to the sergeant, who was listening intently and thought it his duty to nod approval of every remark, as to himself.

'Now where would his knife have been at that moment? It was a pocket flick-knife, the kind a lot of people carry on them. Wait a minute . . .'

He folded back the blade of the knife that was lying on the table with the other exhibits and slipped it into the left-hand pocket of the black trousers.

'No, that makes creases in the wrong place.' He tried the right-hand pocket and seemed satisfied. 'There we are! He has his knife in his pocket. He's alive. And between eleven and twelve thirty at night he died. There's chalk and stone dust on the toes of his shoes. I've found marks left by the same kind of shoes opposite the window, on the wall surrounding Tiburce de Saint-Hilaire's property. Did he take off his jacket to climb the wall? We have to remember that he wasn't a man to make himself comfortable, even at home.'

Maigret was still walking round the room, leaving some of his sentences unfinished and never glancing at the listener sitting motionless on his chair.

'I've found some remnants of burned paper in the fireplace – they'd taken the stove out of it for the summer. Now let's go over the movement he must have made: he takes off his jacket, burns the papers, crushes out the ashes with the foot of that candlestick (I found sweat on the copper), he climbs the wall opposite after getting out over the window-sill, and he climbs back in the same way. Then he takes the knife out of his pocket and opens it. It's not much, but if we knew the order in which those things happened . . . Between eleven and twelve thirty he's back here again. The window is open, and someone shoots him in the head. There's no doubt about that – the bullet came before the knife wound, and it was fired from outside. So Gallet took out his knife. He didn't try to get out, which would suggest that the murderer came into the room, because you don't fight someone seven metres away from you with a knife. And there's more to come: Gallet had half his face blown away. The wound was bleeding, and there's not a drop of blood to be found near the window. The bloodstains we do find show that, once wounded, he moved in a circle with a diameter of no more than two metres. *Severe ecchymosis on left wrist*, writes the doctor who performed the post-mortem. So our man is holding his knife in his left hand, and the murderer seized that hand to turn the weapon against him. The blade pierces his heart, and he falls all at once, dropping the knife. That doesn't bother the murderer, *who knows that it will have only the victim's own fingerprints on it*. Gallet's wallet is still in his pocket; nothing has been stolen from him. However, Criminal Records claims that there are tiny traces of rubber on the travelling bag in particular, as if someone had been holding it with rubber gloves on.'

'Strange! Very strange!' said the delighted sergeant, although he would not have been able to repeat a quarter of what had been said.

'The strangest thing of all is that as well as those traces of rubber they found some powdered rust.'

'Maybe the revolver was rusty!'

Maigret said nothing in reply to this but went to stand

at the window, where, looking somewhat unkempt, with the sleeves of his white shirt billowing out, his outline looked enormous against the lighted rectangle. A thin trail of blue smoke rose in the air above his head. The sergeant stayed in his corner, hesitating even to change the position of his legs.

'Didn't you want to see my vagrants?' he asked timidly.

'Oh, are they still there? You can let them go again.'

Maigret went back to the table, rubbing his hair up the wrong way, tapped the pink file, changed the place of the photos and looked at the other man.

'Did you come on a bicycle? Would you go to the railway station and ask what time Henry Gallet – young man of about twenty-five, tall, thin, pale, dark clothes, horn-rimmed glasses – took the train to Paris on Saturday? And by the way, have you ever heard of a Monsieur Jacob?'

'Only the one in the Bible,' ventured the sergeant.

Émile Gallet's clothes were still on the floor, like the caricature of a corpse. Just as the sergeant was making for the door, someone knocked. It was Monsieur Tardivon, who said, 'Someone to see you, inspector! A lady called Boursang who says she'd like a word with you.'

The sergeant would have liked to stay, but his companion did not invite him to do so. After a satisfied glance round the room, Maigret said, 'Show her in.'

And he leaned down to his insubstantial tailor's dummy, hesitated, smiled, planted the knife in the place where the heart would have been and tamped the tobacco down in his pipe with one finger.

Éléonore Boursang was wearing a pale, well-cut skirt suit, well cut although, far from making her appear youthful, it made her look nearer to thirty-five than thirty. Her stockings fitted nicely, her shoes were well chosen, and her fair hair was carefully arranged under a white straw toque. She was wearing gloves.

Maigret had withdrawn into a shady corner, interested to see how she would present herself. When Monsieur Tardivon left her at the door she stopped, apparently taken aback by the sharp contrasts of light and shadow inside the room.

'Detective Chief Inspector Maigret?' she asked at last, taking a few steps forwards and turning to the silhouette against the window, at whose identity she could so far only guess. 'I'm so sorry to disturb you.'

He came over to her, entering the light. When he had closed the door again, he said, 'Please sit down.'

And he waited. His attitude gave her no help at all; on the contrary, he assumed a cantankerous manner.

'Henry must have mentioned me to you, and so when I found myself in Sancerre I hoped it would be all right to speak to you.'

He still said nothing, but he had not managed to upset her. She spoke with composure, with a certain dignity that almost reminded him of Madame Gallet. A younger Madame Gallet, and no doubt a little prettier than Henry's mother had been, but just as representative of the same social class.

'You must understand my situation. After that . . . that dreadful tragedy, I wanted to leave Sancerre, but Henry wrote a letter advising me to stay here. I've seen you two or three times, and the local people told me that you were in charge of the attempts to track down the murderer. So I decided to come and ask if you had found anything out.

I'm in a delicate situation, given that officially I don't have any connection with Henry or his family . . .'

It didn't sound like a speech she had prepared in advance. The words came easily to her lips, and she spoke with composure. Several times her eyes had gone to the knife placed on the bizarre shape traced by the clothes lying on the floor, but she had not flinched at the sight of it.

'So your lover has told you to pick my brains?' said Maigret suddenly, his voice intentionally harsh.

'He didn't tell me to do anything! He's devastated by what happened. And one of the worst things about it is that I couldn't be at the funeral with him.'

'Have you known him for long?'

She did not seem to notice that the conversation had turned into an interrogation. Her voice remained level.

'Three years. I'm thirty, while Henry is only twenty-five. And I'm a widow.'

'Are you a native of Paris?'

'No, I'm from Lille. My father is chief accountant in a textile factory, and when I was twenty I married a textiles engineer who was killed in an accident by a machine a month after our wedding. I ought to have been paid a pension at once by the firm that employed him, but they claimed that the accident was because of my husband's own carelessness. So as I had to earn my own living, and I didn't want to take a job in a place where everyone knew me, I went to Paris and started work as a cashier in a shop in Rue Réaumur. I brought an action against the textiles factory. The case went on and on through the courts, and it was settled in my favour only two years ago. Once I knew that I would not be in want I was able to leave my job.'

'So you were working as a cashier when you met Henry Gallet?'

'Yes, he's a direct marketing agent, and he often came to see my employers on behalf of the Sovrinos Bank.'

'Didn't the two of you ever think of marrying?'

'We did discuss it at first, but if I had married again before my case was decided in court I wouldn't have been in such a good position over the pension.'

'So you became Henry Gallet's mistress?'

'Yes, I'm not afraid of the word. He and I are united just as much as if we'd gone through a wedding ceremony at the town hall. We've been seeing each other daily for the last three years, and he eats all his meals at my place . . .'

'But he doesn't actually live with you in Rue de Turenne?'

'That's because of his family. They have very strict principles, like my own parents. Henry decided he'd rather avoid friction with his by leaving them in ignorance of our relationship. But all the same it's always been agreed that when there are no more obstacles and we have enough to go and live in the south of France we'll get married.'

She showed no embarrassment even when faced with the most indiscreet questions. Now and then, when the inspector's eyes went to her legs, she simply pulled her skirt down.

'I have to go into all the details. So Henry was eating his meals with you . . . did he contribute to the expenses?'

'Oh, that's very simple! I kept accounts, as you do in any well-organized household, and at the end of the month he gave me half of what had been spent on our food and drink.'

'You mentioned going to live in the south of the country. Was Henry managing to put some money aside?'

'Yes, just like me! You must have noticed that his constitution isn't very strong. The doctors say he needs good fresh air. But you can't live out of doors when you have to earn a living and you don't have a manual job. I love the country too. So we live modestly. As I told you, Henry is a direct marketing agent for Sovrinos – a small bank concentrating mainly on speculation. So he was at the source of it here, and we used everything we could save one way or another to invest on the stock exchange.'

'You have separate accounts?'

'Of course! We never know what the future has in store for us, do we?'

'And what capital have you built up in this way?'

'It's hard to say exactly, because the money is in securities, and they change value from one day to the next. Around 40,000 to 50,000 francs.'

'And Gallet?'

'Oh, more than that! He didn't always like to let me embark on risky speculations like the mines of Plata last August. At the moment he must have about 100,000 francs.'

'Have you decided the figure at which you'll stop?'

'Five hundred thousand . . . we expect to work in Paris for three more years.'

Maigret was now looking at her with feelings verging on admiration. But a particular kind of admiration, with more than a touch of revulsion in it. She was thirty! Henry was twenty-five! They were in love, or at least they had decided to spend their lives together. Yet their relationship was like that of two partners in a business enterprise! She spoke of it simply, even with a certain pride.

'Have you been in Sancerre for long?'

'I arrived on 20 June to stay for a month.'

'Why didn't you go to stay at the Hôtel de la Loire, or the Commercial?'

'Too expensive for me! I'm paying only twenty-two francs a day at the Pension Germain, at the far end of the village.'

'So Henry came on the 25th? What time?'

'He has only Saturday and Sunday off, and it had been agreed that he'd spend the Sunday at Saint-Fargeau. He came here on Saturday morning, and left by the last train that evening.'

'And that was when?'

'Eleven thirty-two p.m. I went to the station with him.'

'Did you know that his father was here?'

'Henry told me he'd met him. He was furious, because he was sure his father had come here just to spy on us, and Henry didn't want his family getting involved in what's no one's business but our own.'

'Did the Gallets know about that 100,000 francs?'

'Of course! Henry has come of age – he had a right to live his own life, didn't he?'

'In what terms did your lover usually speak of his father?'

'He thought poorly of him for his lack of ambition. He said it wasn't right, at his age, for him still to be selling junk jewellery. But he was always very respectful to his parents, especially his mother.'

'So he didn't know that in reality Émile Gallet was nothing but a crook?'

'A crook? Him . . . ?'

'And that for the last eighteen years he hadn't been selling "junk jewellery" at all?'

'That can't be true!'

Was she playing a part as she looked at the lugubrious dummy corpse on the floor with a kind of wonderment?

'I'm stunned, inspector! Him! With his odd ways, his ridiculous clothes? He looked just like a poor pensioner!'

'What did you two do on Saturday afternoon?'

'We went for a walk in the hills, Henry and I. It was when he left me to go back to the Commercial that he met his father. Then we met again at eight and we went for another walk, on the other side of the water this time, until it was time for Henry to catch the train.'

'And you didn't come close to this hotel?'

'It was better to avoid a meeting.'

'Then you came back from the station by yourself. You crossed the bridge . . .'

'And I turned left at once to get back to the Pension Germain. I don't like walking on my own at night.'

'Do you know Tiburce de Saint-Hilaire?'

'Who's he? I've never heard the name . . . Inspector, I hope you don't suspect Henry of anything.' Her expression was animated, but she was as composed as ever. 'I'm here because I know him. He's almost always been ill, and that's made him gloomy and distrustful. We can sometimes spend hours together without talking. It's pure coincidence that he met his father here. Although I realize it might seem an odd coincidence. He's too proud to defend himself . . . I don't know what he told you. Did he answer your questions at all? What I can swear is that he never left me from eight in the evening to the time when he caught his train. He was nervous. He was afraid his mother would hear about our relationship, because he's always been very fond of her, and he foresaw that she'd try to turn him against me . . . I'm not a young girl any more! There are five years between us. And, after all, I've been his mistress. I can't wait to hear that the murderer is behind bars, especially for Henry's sake. He's clever enough to know that his meeting with his father could give rise to terrible suspicions.'

Maigret went on looking at her with the same surprise. He was wondering why this behaviour, which after all did her some credit, did not move him. Even as she uttered those last phrases with a certain vehemence, Éléonore Boursang was still in control of herself. He moved the papers to show a large photo from Criminal Records of the corpse as it had been found, and the young woman's eyes moved over the disturbing image without lingering on it.

'Have you found out anything yet?' she asked.

'Do you know a Monsieur Jacob?'

She raised her eyes to him as if inviting him to see the sincerity in them. 'No, I don't know the name. Who is he? The murderer?'

'Perhaps,' he said, as he went towards the door.

Éléonore Boursang left in much the same way as she had come into the room. 'May I come to see you now and then, inspector, to ask if you have any news?'

'Whenever you like.'

The sergeant was waiting patiently in the corridor. When the visitor had disappeared, he cast an inquiring glance at the inspector.

'What did you find out at the station?' Maigret asked.

'The young man took the Paris train at eleven thirty-two with a third-class return ticket.'

'And the crime was committed between eleven and half

past twelve,' murmured the inspector thoughtfully. 'If you hurried you could get from here to Tracy-Sancerre in ten minutes. The murderer could have done the deed between eleven and eleven twenty. If it takes ten minutes to reach the station, then you wouldn't need any longer to get back ... so Gallet could have been killed between eleven forty-five and half past twelve *by someone coming back from the station* ... Except there's that business of the barred gate! And what the devil was Émile Gallet doing on the wall?'

The sergeant was sitting in the same place as before, nodding his approval and waiting to hear what followed. But nothing followed.

'Come on, let's go and have an aperitif!' said Maigret.

6. The Meeting on the Wall

'Still nothing?'

'. . . *bution!*'

'What word did you say just now?'

'*Preparations*. At least, I suppose so. The *ions* bit is missing. Or it could be *preparation*, singular. Or *preparatory*.'

Maigret sighed, shrugged his shoulders and left the cool room, where a tall, thin, red-haired young man with a tired face and the phlegmatic manner typical of northerners had been bending over a table since that morning, devoting himself to work that would have discouraged even a monk. His name was Joseph Moers, and his accent showed that he was of Flemish origin. He worked in the labs of Criminal Records and had come to Sancerre at Maigret's request, to set up shop in the dead man's hotel room, where he had arranged his instruments, including a strange kind of spirit stove.

He had hardly looked up since seven in the morning, except when the inspector entered the room abruptly or stood at the window looking out on the nettle lane.

'Anything?'

'I . . . you . . .'

'Huh?'

'I've just found an *I* and a *you*, except that the *u* is missing too.'

He had spread out some very thin sheets of glass on

the table, and as he went along with his work was coating them with liquid glue heated on the spirit stove. From time to time he went over to the fireplace, delicately picked up one of the pieces of burned paper and put it on one of the sheets of glass. The ash was fragile and brittle, ready to crumble to bits. Sometimes it took five minutes to soften it by surrounding it with water vapour, and then it was stuck on the glass.

Opposite him, Joseph Moers had a small case which was a veritable portable laboratory. The larger pieces of charred paper measured seven to eight centimetres. The smaller pieces were mere dust.

. . . bution . . . prepara . . . I . . . yo

That was the result of two hours of work, but, unlike Maigret, Moers was not impatient and did not flinch at the thought that he had examined only about one-hundredth of a part of the contents of the fireplace. A large purple fly was buzzing as it circled round his head. It settled on his frowning brow three times, and he didn't even raise a hand to brush it away. Perhaps he didn't even notice it.

However, he did tell Maigret, 'The trouble is that when you come in through the doorway you set up a draught! You've already lost me some ash like that.'

'Oh, all right! I'll come in through the window!'

It was not a joke. He did it. The files were still in this room, which Maigret had chosen as a study, and where the clothes spread on the floor with a knife piercing them had not even been touched. The inspector was impatient to know the result of the expertise he had summoned to his aid, and as he waited he could hardly keep still.

For quarter of an hour, he could be seen walking up and down the lane with his head bent, hands clasped behind his back. Then he straddled the window-sill, his skin burning in the sunlight and shiny; he mopped his brow and growled, 'Slow work, if you ask me!'

Did Moers even hear him? His movements were as precise as a manicurist's, and his mind was entirely on the sheets of glass that he was covering with irregularly outlined black marks.

The main reason why Maigret was agitated was that he had nothing to do, or rather he thought it was better not to try doing anything before he had a clear idea of what was on the paper burned on the night of the crime. And as he paced up and down the lane, where the oak leaves cast dappled light and shade on him, he kept going over the same ideas.

Henry and Éléonore Boursang could have killed Gallet before going to the station, he thought. Éléonore could have come back on her own to kill him after seeing her lover off on the train . . . and then there's that wall, and that key! What's more, there was a certain Monsieur Jacob, the man whose letters Gallet was fearfully hiding . . .

He went back ten times to examine the lock of the barred gate, without finding anything new. Then, as he was passing the spot where Émile Gallet had climbed the wall, he suddenly went into action himself, took off his jacket and put the toe of his right shoe into the first join between the stones. He weighed a good hundred kilos, but he had no difficulty in grasping the hanging branches, and once he had a hold on them it was child's play to finish the climb.

The wall was made of irregular stones covered with a coat of whitewash. On top of it was a row of bricks set edgeways. Moss had invaded them, and there was even grass growing and flourishing.

From his perch, Maigret had an excellent view of Moers deciphering something through his magnifying glass.

'Anything new?' he called.

'An *s* and a comma.'

Above his head the inspector now had not oak leaves, but the foliage of an enormous beech tree, its trunk coming up from the property on the other side of the wall.

He knelt down, because the top of the wall was not wide, and he was not sure of keeping his balance on his feet, examined the moss to right and left of him and murmured, 'Well, well!'

Not that his discovery was sensational. It consisted solely of the fact that the moss had been scuffed and even partly removed at a spot directly above the scratches on the stone, but nowhere else.

As the moss was fragile, as he quickly established, he felt absolutely certain that Émile Gallet had not walked along the wall, not even as much as a metre either way.

So now to find out if he came down on the side of the Saint-Hilaire property . . .

Strictly speaking, this place was not really part of the grounds, no doubt because the area was hidden behind a great many trees and served as a kind of outdoor lumber room. A dozen metres from Maigret, there were piles of old barrels, empty, stove in or minus their hoops. There were also old bottles, several of which had held pharmaceuticals, crates, a decrepit mower, rusty tools and packages of old numbers of a comic magazine tied up with string. Soaked with rain, dried and discoloured by the sun, stained by the soil, they were a sad sight.

Before climbing down from the wall, Maigret made sure that just below him, in fact just below the place that Gallet must have occupied on the wall himself, there were no markings on the ground. He jumped so as not to risk scratching the wall and was rewarded by landing on all fours.

There was nothing to be seen of Tiburce de Saint-Hilaire's villa apart from a few light-coloured patches in the filigree pattern of the foliage. An engine was chugging, and Maigret now knew that it was pumping water from the well into stocks for the household.

This corner of the park was full of flies because of all the rubbish. The inspector had to keep shooing them away, and did so in an increasingly bad temper.

First for the wall, he thought.

The examination of the wall was easy. It had been given a coat of whitewash on both sides in spring. Maigret could see that there was no trace of any mark or scratch underneath the place where Émile Gallet had climbed the wall, and no footprints for ten metres anywhere near.

However, near the casks and bottles the inspector noticed that a barrel had been dragged two or three metres and then stood on end at the foot of the wall. It was still there. He got up on it, and his head came above the top of the wall exactly ten and a half metres from the place where Gallet had been stationed. Furthermore, from where he was he saw Moers still at work, not even taking time off to mop his face.

'Found anything?'

'*Clignancourt* . . . but I think I have a better fragment here.'

The moss on the wall above the barrel had not been torn away, but looked as if it had been crushed by arms pressing on it. Maigret tried leaning on his elbows and got the identical result a little further along.

In other words, he reflected, Émile Gallet gets up on the wall *but does not come down on the side of Saint-Hilaire's property*. On the other hand, someone coming from inside the Saint-Hilaire property hauls himself up on that barrel *but goes no higher and does not leave the enclosure of the grounds, or at least not that way.*

For that to make any sense, the couple going for a nocturnal expedition would have had to be a young man and a girl. And whichever of them had stayed inside the wall could have brought the barrel as close to the other as possible.

But this couldn't have been a lovers' meeting! One of the couple must certainly have been Monsieur Gallet, who had taken off his jacket before embarking on an exercise which was far from compatible with his character.

Was the other one Tiburce de Saint-Hilaire?

The two men had seen each other first that morning, then in the afternoon, quite openly. It was not very likely that they had decided on such a roundabout way of seeing each other again after dark!

And at a distance of ten metres from one another they wouldn't even have been able to hear each other if they spoke in an undertone.

Unless, thought Maigret, they had come separately, first one and then the other . . . but which of the two had hoisted himself up on the wall first? And had the two men met?

It was about seven metres from the barrel to Gallet's room – the distance at which the gun had been fired.

When Maigret turned round he saw the gardener, who was looking at him with an interested expression.

'Oh, it's you,' said the inspector. 'Is your master here?'

'Gone fishing.'

'You know I'm from the police, don't you? Well, I'd like to get out of these grounds without jumping the wall. Would you open the gate at the end of the nettle lane for me?'

'No problem!' said the man, making off in that direction.

'Do you have the key?'

'No, you'll see!' And when he reached the gate he put his hand unhesitatingly into the gap between two stones and cried out in surprise.

'Good heavens!'

'What?'

'It isn't there any more! And I put it back myself last year, that's when three oak trees were chopped down and we got them out this way.'

'Did your master know?'

'Course he did!'

'You don't remember seeing him go that way?'

'Not since last year.'

Another version of the facts automatically began taking shape in the inspector's mind: Tiburce de Saint-Hilaire up on top of the barrel, firing the gun at Gallet, going round by way of the gate, leaping into his victim's room . . .

But it was so improbable! Even supposing that the rusty lock hadn't put up any resistance, it would take three minutes to get along the lane separating the two points. And in those three minutes Émile Gallet, with half his face blown away, had not cried out, had not fallen over, had done nothing but take his knife out of his pocket in case someone came along to attack him! It all sounded wrong! It creaked the way the gate ought to have creaked. Yet it was the only theory that made sense in terms of logical deduction from the material clues!

Anyway, thought Maigret, there was a man on the other side of the wall. That was a definite fact. But nothing indicated that the man was Saint-Hilaire other than the lost key and the fact that the unknown stranger was in his property.

On the other hand, two more people closely connected with Émile Gallet, a couple who might have an interest in his death, were in Sancerre at that moment, and there was no firm alibi to show that they had not set foot in the nettle lane. That couple was Henry Gallet and Éléonore.

Maigret crushed a horsefly that had settled on his cheek and saw Moers leaning out of the window.

'Inspector!'

'Anything new?'

But the Fleming had disappeared into the room again.

Before deciding to go the long way round by the bank again, Maigret shook the gate, and contrary to his expectations it gave way.

'Hey, it's not locked after all!' said the gardener in surprise, leaning over the lock. 'Funny thing, that!'

Maigret almost recommended him not to mention his visit to Saint-Hilaire, but looking the man up and down he thought him too stupid to heed it and decided not to make matters more complicated.

'Why did you call me just now?' he asked Moers a little later.

Moers had lit a candle and was looking through the sheet of glass almost entirely covered with black. 'Do you know a Monsieur Jacob?' he asked, putting his head back to examine his work as a whole with satisfaction.

'Good heavens! What have you found?'

'Nothing much. One of the burned letters was signed Monsieur Jacob.'

'Is that all?'

'Just about. The letter was written on squared paper torn out of a notebook or some kind of register. I've only found a few words on that kind of paper. *Absolutely*, or I suppose so because the *ab* is missing. Then *Monday* . . .'

Maigret waited for more, frowning, teeth clenched on his pipe.

'After that?'

'There's the word *prison* underlined twice. Unless something's lost and the word is *prisoner*. Then there's *cash*, or it could be *cashier*. And there's also a number written in words, *twenty thousand* . . .'

'No address?'

'I told you just now, *Clignancourt*. The trouble is that there's no way I can reconstruct the order of the words.'

'Any clue in the handwriting?'

'There isn't any – it was done on a typewriter.'

Monsieur Tardivon was in the habit of serving Maigret's meals himself, and he did so making a great show of discretion together with a touch of conspiratorial familiarity. Now, before knocking, he called from outside the door, 'A telegram, inspector!'

He very much wanted to enter the room, as Moers and his mysterious work intrigued him. Seeing that the officer was about to close the door again, he asked cheerfully, 'And what can I bring you for lunch, inspector?'

'Nothing,' said Maigret curtly. He had opened the telegram. It was from headquarters in Paris; Maigret had asked for certain information. It said:

Émile Gallet left no will. Estate consists of Saint-Fargeau house, estimated value a hundred thousand with furniture, three thousand five hundred francs deposited in bank.

Aurore Gallet gets life insurance three hundred thousand taken out by husband with Abeille company 1925.

Henry Gallet back at work Sovrinos bank.

Éléonore Boursang out of Paris on holiday in Loire valley.

'Good heavens,' muttered Maigret, looking into space for a moment and then, turning to Moers, said, 'Do you know anything about life insurance?'

'That depends,' said the young man modestly. He was wearing a pair of pince-nez fitting so tightly that his whole face looked contracted.

'In 1925 Gallet was over forty-five. And he had liver trouble. How much a year do you think he had to pay for life insurance worth 300,000 francs?'

Moers moved his lips silently. The arithmetic took him less than two minutes.

'About 20,000 francs a year,' he said at last. 'All the same . . . it can't have been easy to persuade a company to take the risk!'

The inspector cast a furious glance at the portrait photo, still standing on the mantelpiece at the same angle as on the piano in Saint-Fargeau.

'Twenty thousand! And he was spending barely 2,000 a month! In other words, about half of what he was painfully squeezing out of the supporters of the Bourbons!'

His eyes moved on from the photograph to the shapeless black trousers, baggy at the knees and shiny, stretched out on the floor. And he summoned up the image of

Madame Gallet with her mauve silk dress, her jewellery, her cutting voice.

He might almost have been about to ask the photograph, 'Did you love her as much as all that?'

Finally, shrugging his shoulders, he turned to the brightly sunlit wall up which, exactly eight days earlier, Émile Gallet had hoisted himself in his shirtsleeves, his starched shirt-front jutting out of his waistcoat.

'There are still some ashes left,' he told Moers, sounding rather weary. 'Try to find me something else about this Monsieur Jacob. Who's that idiot who said he only knew the Jacob in the Bible?'

A boy with a freckled face had his elbows propped on the window-sill, grinning from ear to ear, as a man's voice called up half-heartedly from the terrace, 'You let those gentlemen get on with their work, Émile!'

'Oh no, not another Émile!' grumbled Maigret. 'At least this one's alive! Whereas the other . . .'

But he had enough control over himself to leave the room without looking at the photograph again.

7. Joseph Moers' Ear

The temperature was still scorching. Every morning, the papers had reports of storms breaking in many different parts of France, but it was three weeks since a drop of rain had fallen in and around Sancerre. In the afternoon, the rays of the sun shone directly into the room where Émile Gallet had stayed, making it uninhabitable.

That Saturday afternoon, however, all Moers did was to lower the cream-coloured blind over the open window. Less than half an hour after lunch, he was leaning over his glass sheets and bits of blackened paper, working with the regularity of a metronome.

Maigret prowled round him for several minutes, touching everything, dragging his feet, looking hesitant. At last he sighed, 'Listen, old fellow, I can't take this any more! I admire you, but you don't weigh as much as I do. I must go and get some fresh air.'

But where could he go on a day like this? There was a little fresh air on the terrace, but he would have to put up with the hotel guests and their children. And it was unusual for half an hour to go by in the café without the irritating click of billiard balls being heard.

Maigret went into the courtyard, half of which was in shade, and called to a young waitress passing by, 'Bring me a lounger, will you?'

'Do you want to sit here? You'll be close to all the noise from the kitchens.'

He preferred that, and the clucking of chickens into the bargain, to other people's conversations. He took his lounger over to near the well, spread a newspaper over his face to protect himself from the flies and was soon overcome by a delightful sleepiness. Little by little, the noise of plates being washed in the scullery became unreal, and the drowsy Maigret escaped his obsession with the late Monsieur Gallet.

Exactly when did he notice what sounded like two loud bangs? They did not entirely rouse him from his torpor, because a dream explaining those misplaced sounds surfaced in his mind . . .

He was sitting on the hotel terrace. Tiburce de Saint-Hilaire was passing by in a bottle-green suit, followed by a dozen long-eared hounds . . .

'Weren't you asking the other day if there's any game to be found in this part of the country?' he said.

Raising his gun to shoulder level, he fired it at random, and a whole flock of partridges looking like autumn leaves fell to the ground . . .

'Inspector! Quick!'

He jumped and saw a chambermaid in front of him.

'It's in the bedroom . . . someone's firing a gun!'

The inspector was ashamed of feeling so heavy. People were already running into the hotel, and he was far from being the first to reach Gallet's room, where he saw Moers standing by the table with both hands over his face.

'Everyone out of here!' he ordered.

'Shall I call a doctor?' asked Monsieur Tardivon. 'Look . . . there's blood!'

'Yes, go!'

Once the door was closed he went over to the young man from Criminal Records. He was feeling remorseful.

'What's the matter, lad?' Although, as he could see, there was blood – blood everywhere! On Moers' hands, on his shoulders, on the sheets of glass and on the floor.

'It's nothing serious, inspector . . . just my ear, look!'

He let go of his left earlobe for a moment, and blood immediately spurted out. Moers was pale, but all the same he tried to smile and above all to stop his jaws moving convulsively.

The shutter was still down, filtering the sunlight and giving the air an orange tinge.

'It's not dangerous, is it? There's nothing like an ear for bleeding . . .'

'Calm down and get your breath back.' For the Fleming's teeth were chattering so much that he could hardly speak.

'I ought not to get myself into such a state,' he said. 'But I'm not used to this sort of thing! I had just got up to fetch some new plates . . .'

He dabbed his wounded ear with his bloody handkerchief, leaning on the table with his free hand.

'And so I was standing just here when I heard a bang. I swear I felt the draught of a bullet passing through the air, so close to my eyes that I thought it had taken my pince-nez off. I flung myself backwards, and then at the same time, at once, I mean after the first shot a second one was fired. I thought I was a dead man . . . there was such a racket in my head, as if my brain were boiling!'

His smile was less forced now.

'Well, as you can see, it was nothing, just a little nick in my ear. I ought to have run to the window, but I simply couldn't move. I thought more shots might be fired – I had no idea what it felt like to be under fire before . . .'

He had to sit down. In some sort of delayed reaction, the shock had hit him, and he had gone weak at the knees. 'Don't worry about me,' he told Maigret. 'Find whoever was firing that gun.'

Drops of sweat suddenly stood out on his forehead, and Maigret, seeing that he was about to faint, ran to the door.

'Tardivon!' he called. 'See to Monsieur Moers here. Has a doctor come?'

'He's not at home. But one of the guests staying here is a male nurse at the Hôtel-Dieu hospital in Paris . . .'

Maigret pulled aside the blind and went out over the window-sill, automatically putting the stem of his empty pipe in his mouth. The nettle lane was deserted, half of it in the shade, the other half vibrant with light and warmth. The Louis XIV gate at the end of it was closed.

The inspector could see nothing unusual about the white wall facing the room. As for footprints, it would be no use looking for any in the dry grass, which, like places where the soil was too stony, did not preserve prints. He made for the bank, where some twenty people had gathered, but hesitated to go any further.

'Were any of you on the terrace when those shots were fired?'

Several voices replied, 'I was!' Their delighted owners stepped forward.

'Did you see anyone starting off along this road?'

'No, no one! Not for the last hour, anyway.'

'I never moved from the spot, inspector!' said a thin little man in a multi-coloured sweater.

'Go back to Mama, Charlot! I was here, inspector. If the murderer had gone along the nettle lane I'd have been bound to see him. It could have been fatal!'

'Did you hear the shots?'

'Everyone did . . . I thought they were hunting in the property next door. I even took a few steps . . .'

'And you didn't see anyone on the road?'

'No one at all.'

'But of course you wouldn't have looked behind every tree trunk.' Maigret did exactly that, to put his mind at rest, and then made for the front entrance of the chateau, where he saw the gardener pushing a wheelbarrow full of gravel along a path.

'Your master's not in, is he?'

'No, he'll be at the notary's place. This is the time of day when they play cards.'

'Did you see him leave?'

'I saw him as clearly as I see you now! It was about an hour and a half ago.'

'And you didn't see anyone in the grounds?'

'Not a soul. Why?'

'Where were you ten minutes ago?'

'Right beside the water, loading up this gravel.'

Maigret looked into his eyes. The man appeared to be telling the truth – in fact he looked too stupid to be telling a plausible lie.

Without bothering about him any more, the inspector went over to the barrel propped against the wall enclosing the property, but he saw no indication that the murderer had gone that way. He had no more luck when he examined the rusty barred gate. It did not look as if it had been opened since he himself had pushed it back into place that morning.

'Yet someone fired a gun, twice!'

The people at the hotel were sitting down again now, but the conversation was general.

'I don't expect it means anything.' Monsieur Tardivon came over to the inspector. 'But I've just heard that the doctor has gone to see Petit, the notary. Should I send someone for him?'

'Where's the notary's house?'

'In the square beside the Commercial.'

'Whose is that bicycle?'

'I don't know, but you can take it ... are you going yourself?'

The bicycle was too small for him, but Maigret mounted it, making the springs of the saddle groan under him. Five minutes later he was setting off a chime of bells at the front door of a huge house, very neat and clean, and an old maidservant in a blue checked apron was looking out at him through a peephole.

'Is the doctor here?'

'Who's it for?'

But a half-open window was flung wide, and a man of jovial appearance holding playing cards in his hands leaned out.

'Is it for the guard's wife? I'm just coming!'

'No, there's a man wounded, doctor! Would you go straight to the Hôtel de la Loire, please?'

'Not another crime, at least I hope not!'

Three other men, sitting at a table with gleaming crystal glasses on it, rose to their feet. Maigret recognized Saint-Hilaire among them.

'Yes, a crime! Come on, quick!'

'Anyone dead?'

'No . . . and make sure you bring something to dress a wound.' Maigret was keeping his eyes on Saint-Hilaire, and he realized that the owner of the little chateau was absolutely thunderstruck.

'One question, gentlemen,' he began.

'Just a moment!' the notary interrupted. 'Why hasn't anyone let you in?'

Hearing this, the maid finally opened the door. The inspector went along a corridor and into the sitting room, where there was a pleasant smell of cigars and well-aged spirits.

'What has happened?' asked the master of the house, a well-groomed old man with silky hair and skin as clear as a baby's.

Maigret pretended not to have heard him. 'Gentlemen, I'd like to know how long you have been playing cards.'

The notary glanced at a pendulum clock. 'A good hour.'

'And none of you has left this room during that time?'

They looked at each other in astonishment.

'Good heavens, no! There are only four of us – just the right number for bridge.'

'Are you *absolutely certain*?'

Saint-Hilaire was crimson in the face.

'Who is the victim?' he asked. His throat was evidently dry.

'An officer from Criminal Records. He was working in the room where the late Émile Gallet had stayed, concentrating on a part of the case involving the identity of one Monsieur Jacob . . .'

'Monsieur Jacob,' repeated the notary.

'Do you know anyone of that name?'

'Why, no. Sounds like a Jewish surname.'

'Monsieur de Saint-Hilaire, I'm going to ask you a favour. I'd like you to move heaven and earth to find the key of that barred gate. If necessary I'll lend you officers to search the villa.'

The owner of the chateau tossed the contents of a glass of spirits down his throat in a single gulp, something that did not escape Maigret's notice.

'I'm sorry to have disturbed you, gentlemen.'

'Won't you take a glass of something with us, inspector?'

'Not now, thank you . . . maybe another time.'

He set off on the bicycle again, turned left and soon came to a rather dilapidated house with a barely legible board outside giving its name: Pension Germain.

It was a poor sort of place, and Maigret doubted its cleanliness. A little boy, not very well washed, was standing in the doorway, where a dog was gnawing a bone picked up from the dusty road outside.

'Is Mademoiselle Boursang here?' he asked.

A woman carrying a baby in her arms appeared at the back of the room. 'She's gone out, same as every afternoon, but you'll probably find her on the hill near the old chateau. She took a book with her, and that's her favourite place.'

'Does this road lead there?'

'Yes, turn right after the last house.'

Halfway up the hillside, Maigret had to get off the bicycle and push it. He was feeling more nervous than he would have liked, perhaps because once again he had the impression that he was on the wrong track.

It wasn't Saint-Hilaire who fired those shots, that's for sure, he told himself. Yet all the same . . .

The road he was following crossed a kind of public garden. On the left, where the ground sloped, a little girl was sitting near three goats tethered to stakes. The road went round a sudden bend, and just above him, a hundred metres uphill, Maigret saw Éléonore sitting on a bench with a book in her hands. He called to the girl, who looked about twelve.

'Do you know the lady sitting up there?'

'Yes, sir.'

'Does she often come to sit on that bench and read?'

'Yes, sir!'

'Every day?'

'I think so, sir, but when I'm at school I don't see her.'

'What time did you arrive here today?'

'Oh, ages ago, sir. I left home as soon as I'd had something to eat.'

'And where do you live?'

'In the house you can see down there.'

It was half a kilometre away, a low-built house with something of the look of a farmhouse about it.

'Was the lady already there then?'

'No, sir.'

'When did she arrive?'

'I can't say exactly, sir, but it would be about two hours ago.'

'And she hasn't moved since then?'

'No, sir.'

'Not even to go for a little walk along the road?'

'No, sir.'

'Does she have a bicycle?'

'No, sir!'

Maigret took a two-franc coin out of his pocket and

put it into the child's hand. She closed her fingers on the coin without looking at it and stayed there motionless in the middle of the road, her eyes following him, as he mounted the bicycle again and rode off towards the village.

He stopped outside the post office and drafted a telegram to Paris.

Urgent. Need to know where Henry Gallet was 15 hours Saturday. Maigret, Sancerre.

'I should let that be for now, old fellow!'

'You told me yourself it was urgent, inspector. Anyway I hardly feel a thing!'

Good man, Moers! The doctor had given his ear a dressing as complicated and thick as if he had six bullets in his head. The sparkling bright glass of his pince-nez looked strange in the middle of all that white linen.

Maigret had not felt anxious about him until seven in the evening, knowing that his injury was not a severe one – and now he found him just where he had spent the morning, in front of his sheets of glass, his candle and his spirit stove.

'I haven't found out anything else about Monsieur Jacob. I've just reconstructed a letter signed *Clément* addressed to I don't know whom, and talking about a present intended for a prince in exile. The word *bution* comes in twice, and *loyalism* once.'

'That's of minor interest now,' said Maigret. For all this was obviously to do with the swindle on which Gallet had embarked. The pink file had provided him with information on that subject, as well as several phone calls to the owners of chateaux and manor houses in the Berry and

Cher areas. At some time or other, probably three or four years after his marriage, and one or two years after his father-in-law's death, Émile Gallet had decided that it would be a good idea to make use of the old documents relating to the *Le Soleil* material that he had inherited.

The journal, its text from the pen of Préjean himself, had a very small print run, reserved almost exclusively for the few who subscribed to it, and it kept the hope of seeing a Bourbon back on the throne of France alive in the hearts of a few country squires.

Maigret had leafed through the *Soleil* material, noticing that half a page was always devoted to subscription lists, sometimes on behalf of an old family that had fallen on hard times, sometimes for the propaganda fund, or again in the cause of celebrating an anniversary worthily.

That was what had given Gallet the idea of swindling the legitimists. He had their addresses, he even knew from the lists what sum of money could be got from them and how to appeal to each of them individually for contributions.

'Have you found the same handwriting on the other papers?' Maigret asked.

'Yes, the same,' said Moers. 'In fact Professor Locard, who trained me, would tell you more. Calm, careful handwriting, but with signs of agitation and discouragement at the ends of words. A graphologist would say unhesitatingly that the man who wrote those letters was ill and knew it.'

'Good heavens, that'll do, Moers! You can take a rest now!'

Maigret was looking at two holes in the canvas blind – the holes made as the bullets passed through it. 'Would you go and sit back where you were just now?'

He had no difficulty in reconstructing the trajectory of the bullets.

'The same angle,' he concluded. 'Firing from the same place on top of the wall . . . good heavens, what's that noise?'

He raised the blind and saw the gardener raking the ground of the path where the nettles and tall grass grew.

'What are you doing?' Maigret called.

'It was my master . . . he told me to . . .'

'Look for the key?'

'That's right!'

'And he sent you to look for it here?'

'He's searching the grounds himself. And the cook and the manservant, they're searching inside the house.'

Maigret abruptly pulled the blind down and alone in the company of Moers again he whistled.

'Well, well,' he said. 'Want to bet, old fellow? He'll be the one who finds the key.'

'What key?'

'Never mind, it would take too long to explain. What was the time when you lowered the blind?'

'As soon as I got back here, about one thirty.'

'And you didn't hear any sounds on the lane outside?'

'I wasn't listening for any. I was absorbed in my work . . . it may look silly, but it's a very delicate job.'

'I know it is, I know! Come to think of it, who could have heard me talking about Monsieur Jacob? The gardener, I think. And Saint-Hilaire, who was out fishing, came home for lunch, changed his clothes and went out for his card game. Are you sure that the handwriting on all the other charred papers belongs to Monsieur Clément?'

'Absolutely sure.'

'Then they're of no interest. The only one that counts is the letter signed by Monsieur Jacob speaking of cash, mentioning Monday and looking very much as if it's threatening the recipient of the letter with prison if 20,000 francs is not received by that day. The crime was committed on Saturday . . .'

Sometimes the rake outside hit a stone.

'It wasn't Éléonore or Saint-Hilaire who fired the shots, it was . . .'

'Well, who'd have believed it!' said the gardener's voice outside.

Maigret smiled with pride and went to raise the blind. 'I'll take that!' he said, holding out his hand.

'If I'd expected to find it here . . .'

'I said I'll take that.'

It was the key, an enormous key, the kind you would never find anywhere except an antique dealer's. Like the lock, it was rusty and had some scratches on it.

'All you have to do is tell your master that you handed it over to me. Off you go!'

'But I . . .'

'Off you go!'

And Maigret pulled the blind down and threw the key on the table.

'You might say that, apart from your ear, we've had a wonderful day. Don't you agree, Moers? Monsieur Jacob! The key! Those two shots and all the rest of it. Well . . .'

'Telegram for you!' announced Monsieur Tardivon.

'What was I saying, old fellow?' the inspector finished, after glancing at the telegram. 'We're going backwards, not forwards. Listen to this:

At three p.m. Henry Gallet was with his mother at Saint-Fargeau. Still there at six p.m.

'So?'
'So nothing! There's only Monsieur Jacob left who could have fired on you, and so far Monsieur Jacob has been as hard to pin down as a soap bubble.'

8. Monsieur Jacob

'Wait a moment, Aurore! There's no point in showing yourself in such a state!'

And a muffled voice replied, 'I can't help it, Françoise. That visit reminds me of the other one a week ago. And the journey . . . oh, you don't understand.'

'What I don't understand is how you can mourn for a man like that, a man who dishonoured you, who lied to you all his life. The only good thing he ever did was to take out life insurance . . .'

'Oh, do be quiet!'

'And there's more! He made you live what was almost a life of poverty, swearing that he earned only 2,000 francs a month. The insurance proves that he was making at least twice that and hiding it from you. Who knows if he wasn't earning even more? If you ask me that man was leading a double life, with a mistress and maybe children somewhere else . . .'

'Oh, please don't, Françoise!'

Maigret was alone in the small sitting room of the house in Saint-Fargeau. The maid had shown him in, forgetting to close the door. The two women's voices came to him from the dining room, where the door, opening on to the same corridor, was also only half closed. The furniture and other items were back in their old places, and the inspector couldn't look at the large oak table without remembering that a few days earlier, covered with a black sheet, it had had a coffin and candles on it.

The atmosphere was dismal, the weather oppressive. There had been a storm during the night, but you could feel that there was more rain to come.

'Why should I keep quiet? Do you think it's none of my business? I'm your sister. Jacques is about to be offered an important political post. Suppose the local people find out that his brother-in-law was a crook?'

'Why did you come, then? You've gone twenty years without . . .'

'Without seeing you, because I didn't want to see him! I didn't hide my opinion when you wanted to get married, and nor did Jacques! When your name is Aurore Préjean, when you have a brother-in-law who's managing director of one of the largest tanneries in the Vosges area and another who's going to be principal private secretary to a government minister, you don't marry a man like Émile Gallet. I mean, the name alone tells you . . . A commercial traveller! I wonder how our father ever gave his consent to it! Or rather, between ourselves, I can guess just what happened. In his last days Father thought of only one thing: how to bring out his journal at all costs – and Gallet had a little money. So it was decided to involve him in *Le Soleil*! Don't you dare to say that's not true! But as for you, sister, you had the same education as me, you even look like Mama, and you chose a man who was nothing. Don't look at me like that! I only want you to understand that you've lost no one to shed tears about! Were you happy with him? Frankly, were you?'

'I don't know . . . I don't know any more.'

'Admit that you had more ambition than that!'

'I always hoped he would try something else. I encouraged him to . . .'

'Might as well try encouraging a pebble! And you resigned yourself to it! You didn't even know that you wouldn't be left in poverty on the day he died! Because but for that insurance . . .'

'He did think of that,' said Madame Gallet slowly.

'That's all we need! To hear you talk, I'll end up thinking you loved him!'

'Hush – the inspector might hear us. I must go in and see him.'

'What's he like? I'll come with you. That will be best, considering the state you're in. And please, Aurore, don't look so miserable. The inspector might think you were his accomplice, that you're sad, that you're afraid . . .'

Maigret just had time to take a step back. The two women came through the communicating door, looking not quite as he had imagined them from the conversation he had just overheard.

Madame Gallet was almost as distant in her manner as at the time of their first interview. As for her sister, who was two or three years younger, with peroxide hair and a heavily made-up face, she made Maigret feel that she had twice Madame Gallet's amount of nerve and pretension.

'Have you found out anything more, inspector?' asked the widow wearily. 'Please sit down. Let me introduce you to my sister, who arrived yesterday from Épinal.'

'Where her husband is a tanner, I think?'

'He owns a number of tanneries, actually,' Françoise corrected him drily.

'Madame was not at the funeral, am I right? And now,

three days ago the newspapers reported that you, Madame Gallet, are to receive a life insurance payment of 300,000 francs.'

He spoke slowly, looking right and left with apparent awkwardness. He had come to Saint-Fargeau for no precise reason, to sniff out the atmosphere and refresh his memory of the dead man. None the less, he would not have been sorry to meet Henry Gallet again.

'I'd like to ask you a question,' he said without turning to the two women. 'Your husband must have known that your marriage to him estranged you from your family.'

It was Françoise who answered. 'That's not true, inspector! At first we welcomed him. Several times, my husband advised him to find another job and offered to help him. It was only when we saw that he would always be someone of low achievement, incapable of making an effort, that we avoided him. He would have shown us in a poor light.'

'What about you, madame?' Maigret asked gently, turning to Madame Gallet. 'You encouraged him to change to a different profession? You blamed his lack of ambition?'

'It seems to me that anything like that belongs to our private life. Isn't it my right to keep that to myself?'

Hearing her just now through the door, Maigret had been able to imagine a woman made more human by her grief. A woman who had abandoned that scornful dignity that he now found neither more nor less robust than on the first day.

'Did your son get on with his father?'

Her sister intervened again. 'Henry will make something of himself! He's a Préjean, although physically he looks like his father. And he did right to get away from that atmosphere when he came of age. He was back at work this morning in spite of that attack of his liver trouble he had last night.'

Maigret looked at the table, trying to imagine Émile Gallet somewhere in this room, but he couldn't do it, perhaps because the inhabitants of this villa never set foot in the sitting room except when they were receiving a formal visit from someone.

'Did you have a message for me, inspector?'

'No . . . I'll leave you now, ladies, with my apologies for disturbing you. However . . . yes, I do have one question. Do you have a photograph of your husband in Indochina? I believe he lived there before his marriage.'

'No, I have no photograph of him then. My husband almost never talked about that time of his life.'

'Do you know what he studied as a young man?'

'He was very clever . . . I remember that he talked to my father about Latin literature.'

'But you don't know the name of the school he attended?'

'All I know is that he was a native of Nantes.'

'Thank you very much. And I do apologize to you once again.'

He picked up his hat and stepped backwards into the corridor, still unable to identify the obscure anxiety he felt each time he set foot in that house.

'I hope my name will not be given to the press, inspector,' said Françoise, in a tone not far from impertinence. 'You may know that my husband is a departmental councillor. He has a great deal of influence in government circles, and as you are an official . . .'

Maigret did not feel brave enough to reply to this. He merely looked her between the eyes and then took his leave, sighing.

As he crossed the tiny garden, escorted by the maid with the squint, he murmured thoughtfully, 'You poor devil, Gallet!'

He briefly stopped at the Quai des Orfèvres to pick up his post, which included nothing bearing on the present case. On coming out of the building he looked in, on the off chance, at the shop of the gunsmith who had examined the bullet taken from the dead man's skull as well as the two that had been aimed at Moers.

'Have you finished examining those bullets?'

'Yes, just this minute. I was going to write the report. All three bullets were fired from the same gun, no doubt about that. An automatic revolver, a precision weapon and one of the latest models, no doubt from the National Factory at Herstal.'

Maigret was feeling gloomy. He shook hands with the gunsmith and hailed a taxi. 'Rue Clignancourt, please.'

'What number?'

'Drop me off at either end of the street, it doesn't matter which.'

On the way he tried to banish from his mind the unpleasant memory of the Saint-Fargeau villa and the conversation between the two sisters. He wanted to concentrate only on the positive aspects of the problem. But as soon as he had put a few simple ideas together, back came the woman Françoise whose husband was a departmental councillor – as she had been careful to point out – and who had come running to Les Marguerites on discovering that Madame Gallet had inherited 300,000 francs.

He would have shown us in a poor light.

And early in the marriage Émile Gallet had been badly

treated, just to get the idea into his head that he must do credit to the Préjeans, like their other sons-in-law. But he was only a commercial traveller in gift items!

Yet he had the courage to sign that life assurance agreement and pay the premium for five years, thought Maigret, intrigued. His feelings were contradictory; he was both attracted and repelled by the complex physiognomy of his murder victim. Did he do it because he loved his wife? She too must have given him a piece of her mind, more than once, about his humble station in life.

Funny sort of household! Funny sort of people, too. But in spite of everything hadn't Maigret felt, for a moment, that Madame Gallet felt genuine affection for her husband? True, he had heard her only through the door. That was all gone when she was in front of him. Once again she had been the pretentious and disagreeable petit bourgeois woman who had talked to him on that first visit of his, and who was very much Françoise's sister.

Then there was Henry, who already had a thoughtful and suspicious expression when he was about to take his First Communion, and who at the age of twenty-two didn't marry Éléonore for fear of losing the pension she might get after her late husband's death! Henry who had suffered an attack of his liver trouble but still went straight back to work!

It began to rain. The taxi driver pulled in to the side of the pavement so that he could put up the top of the car.

The three bullets had been fired from the same revolver – from which one might deduce that they had been fired by the same person. However, neither Henry nor Éléonore nor Saint-Hilaire could have fired the last two shots.

Nor could a vagrant. A vagrant doesn't kill for the sake of killing. He steals, and nothing had been stolen.

The lack of progress in this case, circling round the lacklustre and melancholy figure of the dead man, was getting Maigret down, and it was with a grumpy expression that he entered the first concierge's lodge in the Rue Clignancourt.

'Do you know a Monsieur Jacob?'

'What does he do?'

'No idea. But anyway, he gets letters addressed to that name . . .'

The rain was still falling heavily, but the inspector was quite glad of it, because in this atmosphere the busy road, full of small shops and run-down buildings, was more in tune with his own frame of mind. This traipsing from building to building was a job that could have been given to a junior officer, but Maigret didn't like the idea of getting a colleague mixed up in this case; he couldn't really have said why himself.

'Monsieur Jacob?'

'Not here. Try over there, you'll find some Jews.'

He had popped his head round the door or through the window of a hundred concierge lodges and questioned a hundred concierges, when one of them, a stout woman with tow-coloured hair, looked at him suspiciously.

'What do you want with Monsieur Jacob? You're police, aren't you?'

'Flying Squad, yes. Is he at home?'

'You wouldn't expect him to be at home at this time of day!'

'Where can I find him?'

'In his usual place, of course! Corner of Rue Clignancourt and Boulevard Rochechouart. Here, I hope you're not going to bother him! Poor old fellow like that, I'm sure he never did anyone any harm. So maybe he didn't always have a trading permit – is that why you're here?'

'Does he get a lot of post?'

The concierge frowned. 'So that's what you're here for, eh?' she said. 'I might have known it. Not a nice story, that. You must know as well as me that he only got a letter once every two or three months.'

'By registered post?'

'No, more like a little package than a letter.'

'Containing banknotes, I expect?'

'How would I know?' she said tartly.

'I think you do! Yes, I think you do! You felt those envelopes and you, too, had an idea that there were banknotes inside.'

'And suppose there was? Monsieur Jacob wouldn't have been breaking no bank!'

'Where's his room?'

'His attic, you mean? Right up at the top. He has a hard time getting upstairs every evening with his crutches.'

'Has no one ever come looking for him?'

'Let's see . . . about three years ago. Old gentleman with a pointy beard, looked like a priest without a cassock. I told him, like I told you . . .'

'Was Monsieur Jacob already getting letters?'

'He'd just had one.'

'Did the man wear a close-fitting jacket?'

'He was all in black, like a priest.'

'Doesn't Monsieur Jacob ever have visitors?'

'There's only his daughter, she's a chambermaid in

a furnished place in the Rue Lepic, got a baby on the way.'

'What's his profession?'

'You mean you don't know? And you from the police and all? Are you making fun of me? Monsieur Jacob, why, he's the oldest newspaper seller in the area. Old as the hills, everyone knows him . . .'

Maigret stopped on the corner of Rue Clignancourt and Boulevard Rochechouart, outside a bar called Au Couchant. There was a vendor of peanuts and toasted almonds at the end of the terrace who probably sold chestnuts in winter. On the side of Rue Clignancourt a little old man was sitting on a stool, reciting the names of newspapers in a hoarse voice which was lost in all the noise coming from the crossroads.

'Intran . . . Liberté . . . Presse . . . aris-Soir . . . Intran . . .'

A pair of crutches was propped against the front of his stall. One of the old man's feet had a leather shoe, but he wore only a shapeless slipper on the other.

At the sight of the newspaper seller, Maigret realized that 'Monsieur Jacob' was not his real name but a nickname, because the old man had a long beard divided into two with two pointed ends, and above it was a curved nose in the shape of those clay pipes known as Jacobs.

The inspector suddenly remembered the few words of a letter that Moers had been able to reconstruct: *twenty thousand . . . cash . . . Monday*. And suddenly, leaning over the lame man, he asked 'Have you got the latest consignment?'

Monsieur Jacob raised his head, opening and closing his reddened eyelids several times.

'Who are you?' he asked at last, handing a copy of *L'Intransigeant* to a customer and looking in a box-wood bowl for the right change.

'Police Judiciaire! Now, let's talk nicely, or I'll have to take you away. This is a nasty business.'

Monsieur Jacob spat on the pavement.

'Then what?'

'Do you have a typewriter?'

The old man cackled with laughter, this time spitting out a chewed cigarette end, of which he had quite a collection in front of him already.

'No point playing who's cleverest,' he said in a thick voice. 'You know it's not me. Though I'd have done best to stay away from trouble, for the little I've got out of it.'

'How much?'

'She gave me a hundred sous a letter. So it's a pathetic business.'

'A business likely to land those involved in it in court.'

'You don't say! So they really were notes of a thousand? I wasn't so sure. I felt the envelopes, they made a kind of silky sound. I held them up to the light, but I couldn't see inside, the paper was too thick.'

'What did you do with them?'

'Brought them here. Didn't even need to say when I'd be here ... around five the little lady who bought an *Intran* off of me would turn up without fail, put the hundred sous in the bowl here and slip the package into her bag.'

'A small brunette?'

'No, no, a tall blonde. More strawberry blonde, and ever so nicely dressed, my word, yes! She'd come up out of the Métro ...'

'When did she first ask you to do her this service?'

'It'll be about three years back . . . wait a minute. Yes, my daughter had had her first baby, he was out at Villeneuve-Saint-Georges with a wet-nurse . . . that's right, a little less than three years ago. It was getting late, I'd packed up the merchandise and was hoisting it on my back; she asked if I had a fixed address and if I could help her. We see all sorts around here. Well, so it was about getting letters addressed to me, not opening them, bringing them here in the afternoon.'

'Was it you who fixed the price at five francs a package?'

'It was her . . . I was just pointing out it was worth more – joking, like – what with the price of a litre of red these days, but she started going over to the peanut vendor . . . an Algerian, he is. Some folk'll work for nothing. So I said yes.'

'And you don't know where she lives?'

Monsieur Jacob winked. 'Not so stupid when it comes to it, eh? Even if you are police! There was someone else who tried to find out, early on that was. My concierge only told him I sold my papers here. She described him to me, and I reckoned he was the young lady's father. So he started hanging around when there was a package for me to deliver, but never said a word to me. Yes, wait a minute – he lay low over there, behind the fruit stall. And then he went chasing off after her, but he didn't have any luck. In the end he came to find me and offered me 1,000 francs for the young lady's address. He could hardly believe it when I said I had no more idea than he did. Seems like she led him a fine dance on who knows how many Métro trains and buses, and then she shook him off outside an apartment building with two exits. He wasn't a joker either, that one. I soon caught on that he wasn't her father.

He tried his luck again, twice. I thought I ought to warn my customer, and I reckon she led him on another merry dance, because he didn't try again. Well, and so what else do you think I got instead of that man's 1,000 francs? A whole louis! And I had to pretend I didn't have any change or I'd only have got ten francs, and she went off muttering something that wasn't very polite, though I didn't understand it. She was a sly one! But talk about a cheapskate!'

'When did that last letter arrive?'

'I reckon three months back. You've got to move about a bit in case the customers don't see the papers any more. That all I can do for you, then? You've got to admit I'm the right sort, and I didn't try to do you down . . .'

Maigret put twenty francs in the bowl, made a vague gesture of farewell and walked off with a thoughtful expression. As he passed the entrance to the Métro, he made a face of distaste at the thought of Éléonore Boursang going off with an envelope containing several 1,000-franc notes after throwing five francs to old Jacob, taking ten different Métro and bus lines, entirely at her ease, and to cap it all going through a building with two exits before heading back to her own apartment.

What could that have to do with Émile Gallet taking off his jacket and persisting in climbing a wall three metres high?

Monsieur Jacob, on whom Maigret had pinned his last hopes, was vanishing into thin air.

There was no Monsieur Jacob!

Was he to believe that, instead, there was a couple, Henry Gallet and Éléonore Boursang, who had found out Henry's father's secret and were making him pay for it?

Éléonore and Henry, who hadn't killed anyone!

Saint-Hilaire hadn't killed anyone either, in spite of his contradictions in the matter of the open gate and *the key that he himself had thrown on to the nettle lane, making sure that his gardener found it after the inspector had told him that he was going to get his hands on it at all costs!*

None of that made any difference to the fact that two bullets had been fired at Moers, and that Émile Gallet, whose sister-in-law implied that he was bringing shame on the whole family, had been murdered.

At Saint-Fargeau, they were consoling each other by heaping scorn on him, emphasizing the mediocrity of his character and his life, and by the thought that his death, after all, was worth 300,000 francs.

That morning, Henry had gone to deposit securities with the Sovrinos bank and put the 100,000 francs of savings to good account – the savings which must become 500,000 to allow him to go and live in the country with Éléonore.

While she, finally, as calm as when she was exchanging the newspaper seller's envelope for five francs, was in Sancerre, spying on Maigret, or was coming to see him with an unfurrowed brow and innocent eyes to tell him the story of her life.

And Saint-Hilaire was playing cards with the notary!

The only one absent was Émile Gallet. He was firmly in a coffin, half his face torn away by the bullet, maltreated by the forensic surgeon who had seven guests coming to dinner, a stab wound through his heart, and his grey eyes were open because no one had thought of closing their lids.

'Last avenue on the left, near the old mayor's pink marble monument,' said the verger doing duty as cemetery attendant.

And the undertaker in Corbeil was scratching his head as he looked at an order specifying 'a simple stone, sober lines, good taste, not too expensive but distinguished'.

Maigret had seen a good deal in his time. Yet he tried to consider the possibility that the tall woman with strawberry blonde hair was not necessarily Éléonore Boursang and that, if she was indeed Monsieur Jacob's customer, there was nothing to prove that Henry was her accomplice.

The simplest thing, he thought, would be to show the old man her photograph. That was why he had himself driven to Rue de Turenne, where he was almost sure to find a photograph of the young woman in her apartment.

'Madame Boursang isn't here, but Monsieur Henry is upstairs,' the concierge told him.

Evening was drawing in. Maigret bumped into the walls of the narrow staircase on the way up and opened the door indicated by the concierge without knocking.

Henry Gallet was leaning over a table, doing up a rather large parcel. He gave a start then managed to regain his self-control when he recognized the inspector. However, he could not say anything. His teeth were so firmly clenched that it must have hurt. The change in him after a week was alarming. His cheeks were hollow, his cheekbones jutted. Above all, his complexion was an appalling leaden hue.

'I hear that you had a terrible attack of liver trouble last night,' said Maigret, with more ferocity than he had intended. 'Move over, please.'

The parcel was the shape of a typewriter. The inspector tore off the wrapping paper, took a sheet of white paper out of his pocket, typed a few random words on it, took it out of the machine and slipped it into his pocket. Briefly, the noise of the typewriter had broken the silence in the apartment, where dustsheets covered the furniture and there was newspaper stuck to the windows for the holiday season.

Henry, leaning his elbows on a chest of drawers, was looking at the floor, his nerves so tense that it was painful to look at him.

Maigret, heavy, implacable, went on with what he was doing, opened drawers, searched their contents. Finally he found a photograph of Éléonore. Then, ready to leave, his hat pushed back on the nape of his neck, he stopped for a moment in front of the young man and looked him up and down, from head to foot.

'Is there anything you'd like to tell me?'

Henry swallowed and finally managed to say, 'No.'

Maigret was careful not to arrive at Rue Clignancourt, where Monsieur Jacob was still sitting in front of his newspapers, until an hour later. Did he want one more piece of evidence? Before he was even level with the old man, he saw Henry Gallet's long, discoloured face behind the windowpane of a bistro.

Next moment Monsieur Jacob told him, 'Yes, that's her all right. Got her!'

Maigret went off without a word but cast an aggressive glance at the bistro. He could have gone in and set off another attack of Henry's liver trouble simply by putting a hand on his shoulder.

And never mind that *they* didn't kill him, he thought.

Half an hour later, he was walking through the Préfecture without greeting anyone, and in his office he found a letter from the inspector of indirect taxes in Nevers.

9. *A Farcical Marriage*

If you would care to go to the trouble of paying a discreet visit to my home at 17, Rue Creuse, in Nevers, I will give you some information concerning Émile Gallet that will interest you to a very high degree.

Maigret was in the Rue Creuse. In front of him, in a red and black drawing room, was the inspector of indirect taxes for Nevers, who had introduced himself with a conspiratorial air.

'I sent the maid away! As you will understand, that's for the best. And so far as anyone who may have seen you arrive is concerned, you are my cousin from Beaucaire.'

Was he winking at Maigret to emphasize his every word? Not really; instead of closing one eye at a time he was closing and opening them both, very fast, which ultimately made him look as if he had a nervous tic.

'Are you a former colonial yourself? No? I would have thought . . . well, that's a pity, because it would have been easier for you to understand.'

And he continued to bat his eyelids the whole time and adopted an ever more confidential tone; the expression on his face was simultaneously sly and frightened.

'I myself spent ten years in Indochina, at the time when Saigon didn't yet have wide boulevards like Paris. It was there that I met Gallet . . . and what set me thinking along those lines was the way he was stabbed with a knife, as you will see. I'll bet you've found out nothing yet! And you won't find anything out, because it's a story that only a colonial can understand. A colonial who has seen the *thing itself.*'

Maigret had already placed the tax inspector: he knew that with a man of this kind he must possess his soul in patience, be careful not to interrupt, nod now and then – which after all was the only way to gain time.

'He was a great fellow, our friend Gallet. He was some kind of clerk to a notary who's made his way since then, he's a senator. And he was mad on sport – even took it into his head to form a football team. He'd recruited us all, we couldn't resist him – only there was no other team for us to play against. Well, in short, he liked women even better than football, and there were plenty of chances to meet women out there. Ah, yes, he was a jolly companion. And the tricks he played on the fair sex . . . excuse me, please.'

On silent feet, he made for the door and abruptly flung it open to make sure there was no one on the other side.

'Right, well . . . Once he went too far, and I'm not proud of having played the part of his accomplice, without great enthusiasm, I might add. There was a planter who'd just imported two or three hundred Malay workers, and there were some women and children with them – among others a girl, a little creature who might have been carved from amber. I don't remember her name now. But I do remember I was just finishing reading a book by Stevenson about the natives of the Pacific and I mentioned it to Gallet. It's about a white man who organizes a sham marriage, so that he can enjoy the charms of a wild native girl. And my friend Émile got rather carried away by the idea! In those days the Malays couldn't read, in particular the poorer sort who were transported round the place like brute beasts. So Gallet goes to put his request to the girl's father. He decks out his future in-laws in ridiculous garments, he gets together a wedding procession to lead the happy couple to this run-down little house that we'd repaired. Another friend played the part of mayor to marry them. He's dead now, although there'll be others still alive who remember the joke. He was a great joker, Gallet was, and he made sure the whole farce was as comic as possible. The speeches would have had you rolling in the aisles, and the marriage certificate, which we solemnly handed over to the girl, was complete gobbledegook from start to finish. What larks – at the expense of the head of the family, the witnesses and everyone else!'

The inspector of indirect taxes fell silent for a moment, to assume an expression of greater gravity.

'Well, then,' he concluded. 'Gallet lived with the girl as man and wife for three or four months. Then he went back to France, of course leaving the wife who wasn't his wife behind. We were still young, or we wouldn't have made such a joke of it, because the Malays don't forgive easily . . . you don't know them, inspector. The girl waited a long time for her husband to come back. I don't know what happened to her after that but years later I met her again – she'd aged a lot – in a poor quarter of Saigon. And when I read Gallet's name in the local Nevers newspaper . . . I hadn't seen him for twenty-five years, remember. I hadn't even heard anyone speak of him. But it was that knife wound, you see. Can you guess now? It was vengeance, sure enough. A Malay will go all round the world to get revenge. And they're used to knives. Suppose a brother of the girl, or even a son, more civilized now ... suppose he began by using a revolver, because it's a practical weapon. But then instinct got the upper hand.'

Maigret was waiting, with a gloomy expression, listening with only half an ear to this torrent of words. It would be useless to interrupt. In a criminal case there are usually a hundred witnesses of the tax inspector's calibre, and if this time only one turned up it must be because the Parisian newspapers had devoted only a few lines to the case.

'Are you with me, inspector? You'd never have guessed, would you? I thought it better to ask you to come here, because if the murderer knew I was talking to you ...'

'You were saying that Gallet used to play football?'

'He was mad about it! And what a joker! The best company you could find. Why, he was capable of telling funny stories all evening without giving you time to get your breath back.'

'Why did he leave Indochina?'

'He said he had ideas of his own, and they didn't include living on less than 100,000 a year – that was before the war. A hundred thousand francs! You see what I mean? Folk might laugh at him, but he was perfectly serious. He used to laugh and say, "We'll see, we'll see!" He didn't get his 100,000 a year, did he? Now as for me, it was the fevers sent me away from Asia. They still give me shaking fits. You'll take something to eat and drink, won't you, inspector? I'll serve you myself, because I sent the maid out of town for the whole afternoon.'

Maigret did not feel up to accepting the tax inspector's hospitality, or to having to put up with any more of his knowing winks as he launched once again into his story of the vengeful Malay. He could hardly manage to thank the man with a smile – a pallid, civil smile.

Two hours later, he got off the train at Tracy-Sancerre station, where he already knew his way around. As he walked down the road leading to the Hôtel de la Loire, he was in the middle of a soliloquy:

'So suppose this is Saturday 25 June. And suppose I am Émile Gallet. The heat is stifling, my liver is giving me trouble. And in my pocket I have a letter from Monsieur Jacob threatening to tell the police everything if I don't give him 20,000 francs in cash on Monday. My legitimists would never come up with 20,000 francs at a time. The average amount I manage to get out of them is between 200 and 600 francs – very rarely 1,000! I get to the Hôtel de la Loire and I ask for a room *looking out on the courtyard* . . . why the courtyard? Because I'm afraid of being murdered? By whom?'

He was walking slowly with his head bent, trying hard to get inside the dead man's skin.

'Do I know who Monsieur Jacob really is? He's been blackmailing me for three years, I've been paying up for three years. I've interrogated the newspaper seller on the corner of Rue Clignancourt. I've followed a young blonde who shook me off at a building with two exits. I can't possibly suspect Henry because I know nothing about his affair. Nor do I know that he's already saved 100,000 francs and needs 500,000 to go and live down south. Which means that Monsieur Jacob remains a terrifying lurking entity behind the figure of the old street seller.'

He made a gesture like a teacher wiping the exercise off a blackboard with a duster. He would have liked to forget all he now knew and start his investigation again from scratch.

Émile Gallet was a jolly fellow. He made his friends form a football team.

He passed the hotel without going in and rang the bell at the main entrance to the Saint-Hilaire property. Monsieur Tardivon, who was standing in his doorway and whom Maigret had not greeted, watched him go disapprovingly.

The inspector had to wait some time out in the road. At last a manservant opened the door, and Maigret asked, point-blank, 'How long have you been living in this house?'

'A year . . . but isn't it Monsieur de Saint-Hilaire you want to see?'

Monsieur de Saint-Hilaire himself gave Maigret a friendly wave from a ground-floor window. 'Well now, that key! We had it after all! Won't you come in a moment? How are the inquiries coming along?'

'How long has the gardener been working for you?'

'Oh, three or four years . . . but do come in!'

The owner of the chateau too was struck by the change that had come over Maigret. His features were hard, there was a frown on his brow, and his eyes had a disturbing look of lassitude and malice.

'I'll just get a bottle brought in and we . . .'

'What became of your old gardener?'

'He has a bistro a kilometre from here, on the Saint-Thibaut road. An old rogue who made his pile out of me before setting up on his own account.'

'Thank you.'

'Are you going?'

'I'll be back.'

He seemed to say that without a moment's thought, and with his mind preoccupied went back to the gate and off towards the main road.

So he needed 20,000 francs in a hurry, Maigret went on thinking. He didn't try getting it out of his usual victims, that's to say the local landowners. Saint-Hilaire was the only one he visited. Twice in the same day! Then he climbed the wall . . .

He interrupted himself with an oath. 'Good lord above! And why, in that case, did he ask for a room *looking out on the yard*? If he'd got one, he couldn't have climbed the wall.'

The former gardener's bistro was near a lock on the canal joining the River Loire from the side, and was full of bargees.

'Can you help me, please? Police. I'm inquiring into the crime at Sancerre. Do you remember seeing Émile Gallet visiting your old boss when you worked for him?'

'You mean Monsieur Clément? That's what we called him. You bet I did!'

'Often?'

'Can't really say . . . maybe about once every six months. But that was enough to leave the boss in a bad mood for a couple of weeks.'

'Were his first visits long ago?'

'At least ten years ago, maybe fifteen. Can I offer you a glass of something?'

'No thank you. Did they sometimes argue?'

'Sometimes, no! Every time, yes! I even saw them come to blows like a couple of dockers!'

And yet, Maigret reasoned a little later, as he walked back to the hotel, it wasn't Saint-Hilaire who carried out the killing. First, he couldn't have fired those two shots at Moers, because he was playing cards at the notary's house. And then, on the night of the crime, why would he have gone the long way round by the barred gate?

He saw Éléonore not far from the church but turned his head away so as to avoid her. He didn't want to talk to anyone, her least of all. He heard rapid footsteps behind him and saw her catch up with him. She was wearing a grey dress, and her hair was smooth and tidy.

'Excuse me, please, inspector.'

He turned abruptly and looked her in the eyes with such an aggressive expression that it took her breath away for a moment.

'I only wanted to know whether . . .'

'No, nothing! I've found out nothing at all!'

And he walked away without another word, hands behind his back.

Suppose the room looking out on the courtyard had been free, he wondered, would he be dead just the same?

A little boy playing with a football collided clumsily with the inspector's legs. Maigret picked him up and put him down a metre away without even looking at him.

Anyway, he continued his train of thought, he didn't have the 20,000 francs. He couldn't get them together in time for Monday. And he couldn't have climbed the wall. It would have been impossible to fire on him from that wall. So, Maigret reasoned, *he wouldn't be dead now*!

He mopped his brow, although the temperature was much more tolerable than the week before. He had that annoying feeling of being close to the solution that he wanted, yet unable to reach it.

He had a great many facts: that business of the wall, the two gunshots fired a week later at Moers, the conduct of Monsieur Jacob, the visits to Saint-Hilaire fifteen years before, the lost key so providentially found by the gardener, the matter of the hotel room, the knife wound finishing off the work of the bullet with a few seconds between them, and finally the football team and the farcical marriage . . .

For Gallet's passion for sport, his funny stories and his amorous exploits were all that could be gleaned from the rambling tale of the inspector of indirect taxation.

A jolly companion . . . liked women even better than football . . .

'Will you be dining on the terrace, inspector?' asked Monsieur Tardivon.

Maigret had got there without noticing it. 'I don't mind one way or the other.'

'And how is your case getting on?'

'Let's say it's over.'

'What? Then the murderer is . . . ?'

However, the inspector passed him, shrugging his shoulders, went down the corridors full of cooking smells and went into the room where his files were still heaped on the table, the mantelpiece and the floor.

No one had touched the clothes representing the dead man. Maigret bent down, removed the knife from where it was stuck in the floor and began fingering it as he walked up and down.

The sky was covered with grey clouds, and by way of contrast the white wall opposite looked dazzling.

The inspector went from the window to the door, from the door to the window, sometimes glancing at the photograph on the mantelpiece.

'Come here a moment!' he suddenly said as he reached the window, perhaps for the thirtieth time.

The leaves shook above the wall, where Maigret had made out the poorly concealed face of Saint-Hilaire.

The owner of the chateau, whose first movement had been to shrink back, trying to make light of it but nevertheless sounding anxious, asked, 'You want me to jump?'

'No, come the long way round through the gate. It's easier.'

The key was on the table, and Maigret nonchalantly tossed it over the wall as he went on walking up and down the room. He heard the key fall on the other side among the collection of jumble. Then came the noise of the barrel being moved, and more sounds from the foliage and branches.

Saint-Hilaire's hand must have been shaking, for the key clicked against the lock for some time before Maigret heard the squealing hinges of the gate. However, when the owner of the little chateau reached the window he had his self-confidence back, and it was in a jovial voice that he said, 'Well, nothing escapes your eagle eye! I find this case of yours so fascinating that, when I saw you coming in, I had the idea of spying on you to get as good a view as yours, and then intrigue you at our next meeting . . . Shall I come round through the hotel?'

'No, no, come through the window!'

Saint-Hilaire did so easily, commenting as he looked round the room, 'How strange! The atmosphere in which you reconstruct what happened . . . those clothes. Did you arrange this spectacle?'

Maigret filled his pipe exaggeratedly slowly, tapping each pinch of tobacco down with his forefinger a dozen times. 'Do you have a match?'

'No, I use a lighter. I don't like matches.'

The inspector's eyes went to three pieces of greenish wood, burned at one end, lying beside the ashes of paper in the hearth.

'Yes, of course,' he said, not indicating what it was he approved of.

'You wanted to ask me something?'

'I'm not sure yet. I saw you . . . and as I am all at sea, I thought that an intelligent man might give me some ideas.'

He perched on the corner of the table and held out the bowl of his pipe to the lighter in his companion's hand.

'Well, so you're left-handed!'

'Me? Oh no, not at all. Just chance. I can't think why I'm offering you my lighter in my left hand.'

'Would you close the window? If you would be so kind.'

Maigret, never taking his eyes off the other man, noticed a hesitation in Saint-Hilaire's movements as, obviously paying great attention to what he was doing, he used his right hand to turn the window catch.

10. *The Assistant*

'Open the window.'

'But you've just asked me to . . .'

And Tiburce de Saint-Hilaire smiled, as if to say, 'Of course, whatever you say . . . I'm sorry if I expressed myself badly.'

Maigret himself was not smiling. If you had seen his face, you would probably have described the predominant impression as boredom. His gestures and tone of voice were gruff, he walked with a staccato step, and also in a staccato style he raised and lowered his head, picked up an object from one place to put it down in another, for no reason at all.

'Since the case fascinates you so much, I'll take you on as an assistant. So I won't wear kid gloves, and I shall treat you like one of my officers. Call Tardivon, will you?'

Saint-Hilaire did as he was told, opened the door and called, 'Tardivon! Hey there, Tardivon!'

When the hotelier came up Maigret, sitting on the ledge of the window-sill, was looking at the floor. 'A simple question, Monsieur Tardivon. Was Gallet left-handed? Try to remember.'

'Well, I never noticed. It's true that . . . Does a left-handed person shake another person's left hand?'

'Of course!'

'Then he wasn't. I mean, I'd be sure to have noticed. My guests here usually shake hands with me.'

'Go and ask the waitresses. They may have noticed that detail.'

While the hotelier was out of the room, Saint-Hilaire said, 'You seem to think this matter very important?'

But without replying the inspector went out into the corridor and called to Monsieur Tardivon, 'And while you're about it get someone on the line for me: Monsieur Padailhan, inspector of indirect taxation in Nevers. I think he has a telephone.'

He retraced his steps without so much as a glance for his companion, and spent a moment walking round the clothes spread out on the floor.

'And now to work! Let's see – Émile Gallet was not left-handed. In a moment we'll find out if that detail is any use to us. Or rather . . . take that knife. It's the one used in the crime. No – give it to me. There you go, using your left hand again. There! Now suppose that, being attacked, I have to defend myself. And let's remember I'm not left-handed, so of course I hold the handle of the knife in my right hand. Come over here. It's you I'm lunging at. You're stronger than me, you grab my wrist . . . . Go on, grab it! Good, so it's obvious that it's the hand holding the knife you want to immobilize. That'll do. Now, look at this photo of the body, it comes from Criminal Records. And what do we see? It's on the wrist of the *left hand* that Émile Gallet had ecchymosis.'

Maigret broke off. 'What is it, Tardivon? Nevers already? No? You say the waitresses all agree that Gallet wasn't left-handed. Thanks, you can go.'

'And now,' he went on, 'it's just the two of us, Monsieur de Saint-Hilaire. How would *you* explain that? Gallet was not left-handed, yet he held his knife in his left hand! And an examination of the scene shows that there was nothing in his right hand. I see only one solution to the problem. Watch this. I want to plunge that knife into my opponent's heart. What do I do? Follow my slightest gesture. I grab the sleeve over my left hand, because that hand is not going to be any use except to keep the knife pointing the way I want. My right hand is the stronger. It's the one I use to press the left one. Look! This movement . . . I hold my left wrist in the fingers of my right hand. I press very hard, because I'm feverish and it's a case of resisting the pain. I do it so well that I leave ecchymosis on myself.'

And he dropped the knife on the table with an offhand gesture.

'Of course, to accept that reconstruction of the facts we must also admit that Gallet killed himself. And he didn't have an arm long enough to fire at himself from a distance of seven metres from his face, did he? All in good time . . . let's try to find some other explanation!'

The same rather forced smile was still on Saint-Hilaire's lips. But the pupils of his eyes, looking larger than usual, were darting about with unusual mobility so as not to leave Maigret for a moment. Maigret himself was coming and going the whole time, making about fifty vague gestures for every useful one, picking up the pink file, opening it, closing it again, slipping it under a green file, then suddenly going to change the position of one of the dead man's shoes.

'Come with me . . . yes, over the window-sill. So here we are in the nettle lane. Let's suppose it is Saturday evening, it is dark, we can hear the sounds of the funfair and the rifle range. Perhaps we can even see the lights of the carousel with its wooden horses. Émile Gallet, having taken off his close-fitting jacket, hauls himself up to the top of this wall, not an easy thing for a man of his age to do, and he's also worn down by illness. Follow me.'

He made Saint-Hilaire go over to the barred gate, opened it and then closed it again.

'Give me the key. Right, this gate was locked, and as usual the key was in the gap you can see between two stones there. Your gardener himself told me about it. And now we're on your property. Don't forget, it's dark. And take note of this: we are only looking for the meaning of certain clues, or rather we are trying to reconcile contradictory clues. This way, please. Now, imagine someone in this park who is worried by what Émile Gallet is doing. There must be some people who feel like that about him. Gallet is a crook with God knows what else on his conscience. So on this side of the wall we have a man like you and me, a man who has noticed that in the course of the evening Gallet was nervous and who may know that he is in a desperate situation. Our man, whom we will call X, as if he were part of an algebraic equation, comes and goes along the wall and suddenly he sees the outline of Émile Gallet, alias Monsieur Clément, get up on top of the wall without his jacket on. Can this part of the wall round the property be seen from the villa?'

'No. I really don't understand what you're . . .'

'Getting at? Oh, nothing, we're pursuing our inquiries, ready to change track to a hundred different hypotheses if necessary – and wait! I'm switching to another track already. X isn't walking, he's caught sight of some empty barrels and, rather than climbing the wall to see what's happening on the other side of it, he's dragged over one of those barrels to give him a leg up. It's at this moment that the silhouette of Émile Gallet is outlined against the sky. The two men don't speak, because if they'd had anything to say to each other they'd have come closer. You have to raise your voice to be heard from ten metres away. And men meeting in such unusual circumstances, one of them on a barrel, the other balancing on a wall, wouldn't want to attract attention. Besides, X is in shadow. Émile Gallet doesn't see him. He comes down from his perch on the wall, goes back to his hotel room and . . . and here it gets more difficult. Unless we suppose that it was X who fired the shot.'

'What do you mean?'

Maigret, who had climbed up on the barrel, got off it again heavily.

'Give me a light, please. Ah, your left hand again! Now, without wondering who fired the shot, we're going to follow the path taken by our friend X. Come along. He takes the key out of the gap in the wall. He opens the barred gate. But first he has gone somewhere to find a pair of rubber gloves. You'll have to ask your cook if she happens to wear rubber gloves for preparing vegetables, and if so whether they've disappeared. Is she vain?'

'I really don't see what that has to . . .'

Thunder rolled in the distance, but not a drop of rain fell.

'Let's go through. The gate is open now. X approaches the window and sees the corpse . . . because Émile Gallet is dead! The knife wound was inflicted *directly after* the gunshot; that's what the doctors say, and the bloodstains prove it. We saw just now that the knife wound looked just as if it had been inflicted by the victim himself. There are burned papers in the hearth of the room, still warm. And we find some of Gallet's matches there. However, friend X searches the case, and very likely Gallet's wallet as well. He puts it carefully back in Gallet's pocket and leaves the hotel room, but forgetting to lock the gate and to put the key back in its place.'

'And yet the key was found in the grass . . .'

Maigret, who for some time had not looked at the man who now spoke to him, noticed his downcast air.

'Come on . . . that's not all. I don't think I've ever known a case that was so complicated and so simple at the same time. We know, don't we, that the man known in these parts as Monsieur Clément was a crook? And now we see that he himself destroyed all traces of his criminal activities, as if he were expecting some important or indeed some major event . . . yes, this way! Here's the hotel courtyard, and on the left is the room that Émile Gallet said he wanted on the Saturday afternoon – the one he couldn't have because it wasn't vacant. Now, in the afternoon he was in the same situation as in the evening. At all costs he must have 20,000 francs on Monday morning, or whoever was blackmailing him would hand him over to the police. Just suppose he *had* managed to get that room. He couldn't have crossed the nettle lane and climbed the wall. So it was not a *necessity* for him to go along that wall. Or if you prefer, *it could be replaced by something else, something that the courtyard provided*. Now then,' Maigret continued, 'what do we see in that courtyard? A well! You will tell me, perhaps, that he felt like throwing himself into it. But in reply to that, I would tell you that if he left the room he was occupying he could go along the corridor and drown himself all the same. So he needed *the combination of a well and a room* . . . yes, what is it, Monsieur Tardivon?'

'Nevers on the telephone for you.'

'The inspector of indirect taxation?'

'That's right.'

'Come on, Monsieur de Saint-Hilaire. Since you want to help me, it's only fair that you are present at all stages of my inquiries. Take the receiver . . . Hello? Detective Chief Inspector Maigret speaking! Don't worry, I only want to ask you a question that I didn't think of just now. Was your friend Gallet left-handed? You say he was? And he also preferred to use his left foot? He played outside left at football? You're certain of that, are you? No, that's all . . . oh, one detail. Did he know Latin? Why do you laugh? . . . A dunce? . . . As bad as that, was he? It's a strange thing, yes . . . Did you see the photo of the body? . . . You didn't? Well, of course he'd have changed since those days in Saigon . . . the only photo I have was taken when he was on a diet . . . but perhaps, one of these days, I'll show you someone who looks like him. Thank you . . . yes.'

Maigret hung up, uttered a laugh that was especially devoid of any humour and sighed.

'You see how easily one can get carried away! All we've been saying so far depends on one fact, which is that our Émile Gallet is not left-handed. Because if he is left-handed, he could turn the knife against his attacker. What it is to believe the word of a hotelier and the waitresses who work for him!'

Monsieur Tardivon, who had heard that, looked offended. 'Dinner is served,' he announced.

'I'll be with you soon. Might as well finish this . . . especially as I'm afraid of trying the patience of Monsieur de Saint-Hilaire. Let's go back to what they call the scene of the crime, shall we?'

★ ★ ★

Once there, he suddenly asked, 'You saw Émile Gallet in his lifetime. What I'm about to tell you may make you laugh ... yes, by all means put the light on. With this gloomy sky, darkness seems to fall an hour earlier than usual. Well now, I never saw him alive, and since his murder I've been spending my time trying to imagine him. To that end I've come to where I could breathe the air he used to breathe, I've rubbed shoulders with those he used to know ... Look at this portrait photograph, and I bet you'd say, as I do, that he looks a sorry sight. Especially when you know that his doctor gave him only three years to live. His liver was killing him! And he had a weak heart just waiting for an excuse to stop beating. I'd have liked to see Gallet in time as well as space. Unfortunately I can find out nothing about him until after the time of his marriage, because he was always unwilling to talk about his life before it, even to his wife.

'All she herself knows,' Maigret continued, 'is that he was born in Nantes and lived in Indochina for several years. Although he brought back no photograph, not so much as a souvenir – and he never talks about those days. He's a commercial traveller of no importance, a man with some 30,000 francs to his name. When he was thirty he was already clumsy, narrow-minded, melancholy. Then he meets Aurore Préjean and takes it into his head to marry her. The Préjeans have a high opinion of themselves. The girl's father is in dire straits: he can't find the funds to keep his journal going, but he was once private secretary to a claimant to the throne of France. He corresponds with princes and dukes. His youngest daughter is married to a master tanner. In that company our friend Gallet cuts a sorry figure, and if the family accepts him it is surely because he consents to invest his small capital in the journal, *Le Soleil*.'

Maigret went on with the tale of the family as he saw it.

'The Préjeans do not care for him. Having a son-in-law who sells silver-plated giftware is a step down in the world for them. They try to rouse higher ambitions in him. He resists that idea. He does not feel that he is made for a career that would bring him prestige. He already has liver trouble. He dreams of a peaceful life in the country with his wife, whom he deeply loves. But he cannot please her either. Don't her sisters have the audacity to treat her as a poor relation and pour scorn on her marriage?

'Then her father, old Préjean, dies. *Le Soleil* is done for. Émile Gallet goes on selling his shoddy gifts to the peasants of Normandy. And after his weeks of work he consoles himself by going fishing, inventing ingenious devices, and taking watches and alarm clocks apart. His son inherits his physique and his liver trouble, but he has the ambitions of the Préjeans. So much so that one fine day Émile Gallet decides to try something. He has the records of *Le Soleil*. He finds out that many people used to donate various amounts of money if you mentioned the legitimist cause of the rightful king to them. And he tries his hand. He doesn't tell anyone else about it. At first he probably carries on working as a commercial traveller, as a front for his still hesitant criminal activities. But they are what earns him more. Fairly soon he can even buy a plot on the Saint-Fargeau site and have a villa erected on it. He brings his good qualities of order and punctuality into his new way of life. As he is terrified of his wife's family, so as far as she and they are concerned he is still working in Normandy for the firm of Niel.

'He doesn't make a fortune. The legitimists don't have

access to millions, and some of them are slow on the uptake. But at last he is living comfortably enough, and Gallet would be content with that if the family hadn't been blaming him, even under his own roof, for his unambitious ideas. He loves his wife, for all her faults. Perhaps he even loves his son.

'The years pass by. His liver trouble gets worse. Gallet has attacks that make him foresee a premature death. At that point he takes out life insurance for a large sum of money, so that after his death his nearest and dearest will be able to go on leading the same life. He goes to endless trouble . . . Monsieur Clément steps up his visits to the provincial manor houses, where he pesters the dowagers and gentlemen of the *ancien régime* . . . I hope you follow me?

'Three years ago, a certain Monsieur Jacob writes to him. This Monsieur Jacob knows the nature of his work and wants money every two months, a continuous flow of it, as the price of his silence. What can Gallet do? He has brought shame on the Préjean family, he is the poor relation to whom they send a New Year card, but none of his brothers-in-law, who are making their way in the world, want to meet him.

'On Saturday 25 June he is here, with the last letter from Monsieur Jacob in his pocket. It demands 20,000 francs on the following Monday. Obviously you don't come by 20,000 francs in a day by knocking on the doors of legitimists even on the most ingenious of pretexts. And anyway, he doesn't try to. He goes to see you. Twice! After his second conversation with you he asks for a room looking out on the courtyard. Did he have any hope of getting those twenty banknotes for 1,000 francs each out of you? If so, that evening all hope was gone.

'So tell me, what was he going to do in that room that he was unable to get, and then we shall know why he climbed up on the wall!'

Maigret did not raise his eyes to the other man, whose lips were trembling.

'An ingenious theory!' said Saint-Hilaire. 'But . . . especially where I am concerned, I really don't see what . . .'

'How old were you when your father died?'

'Twelve.'

'Was your mother still alive?'

'She died soon after my birth. However, I'd be interested to know what . . .'

'Were you brought up by other relations?'

'I have no other relations. I am the last of the Saint-Hilaires. When he died my father only just had the money to pay for my keep and my studies at a school in Bourges until I was nineteen. But for an unexpected legacy from a cousin whose existence everyone had forgotten . . .'

'And who lived in Indochina, I believe?'

'In Indochina, yes. A distant relation who didn't even bear our name. A Duranty de la Roche.'

'At what age did you get this legacy?'

'I was twenty-eight.'

'So that from the age of nineteen to twenty-eight . . .'

'I had a hard time, yes. I don't blush to say so, far from it. Inspector, it's getting late. Wouldn't it be better if we . . .'

'Just a moment. I haven't yet shown you what can be done with a well and a hotel bedroom. You don't have a revolver on you, I suppose? Never mind, I have mine. There must be some string around somewhere. Right, follow my movements. I tie this string to the butt of the weapon. Let's suppose it measures six or seven metres, or more, that's of no importance. Now, go and find me a large pebble in the road.'

Once again Saint-Hilaire was quick to obey and brought back the stone.

'Your left hand again,' Maigret commented. 'Never mind that. So I tie this pebble firmly to the other end of the string. We can have our demonstration here, if we suppose that the window-sill is the rim of the well. I let my stone down on the other side of it. Yes, that's right, into the well. I have the revolver in my hand. I aim at something, never mind what. Myself, for instance . . . Then I let go. And what happens? The stone, which is dangling above the water, goes down to the bottom of the well, taking with it the string and the revolver tied to the other end. The police arrive to find a dead body, but no trace of a weapon . . . and what do they deduce from that?'

'A crime has been committed!'

'Very good,' said Maigret, and without asking for his companion's lighter he lit his pipe with matches taken from his pocket.

As he picked up Gallet's clothes, with the look of a man pleased with a long day's work, he said in the most natural voice imaginable, 'So now go and find me the revolver.'

'But . . . but you didn't let go of it. You're holding it in your hand.'

'I mean go and find me the revolver that killed Émile Gallet. And hurry up about it.'

So saying, he hung the trousers and waistcoat on the hook in the room, beside the close-fitting jacket with its shiny elbows that was hanging there already.

11. A Commercial Affair

Now that Maigret's back was turned to him, Saint-Hilaire no longer kept firm control of the expression on his face, and a strange mixture of anxiety, hatred and, in spite of everything, a kind of self-assurance could be seen on it.

'What are you waiting for?'

He decided to go out through the window, walked over to the barred gate in the nettle road and disappeared into the grounds, all so slowly that the inspector, slightly worried, strained his ears to hear him.

It was the time of day when you could see, on the riverbank, the luminous halo of light from the terrace, where knives and forks clicked on plates, accompanied by the muted murmuring of the hotel guests' voices. Suddenly branches moved on the other side of the wall. The darkness was so complete that Maigret could hardly make out the figure of Saint-Hilaire on top of it. Another creaking of branches. A voice calling softly. 'Would you like to take it?'

The inspector shrugged his shoulders and did not move, so that his companion had to make the same journey in reverse. When he was in the hotel room again he firstly put a gun on the table. He had straightened his back, and he touched Maigret's arm with an almost casual, albeit slightly gauche, gesture.

'What would you say to two hundred thousand?' He

had to cough. He would have liked to act the *grand seigneur*, completely at ease, but at the same time he felt himself blushing, and there was an obstruction in his throat. 'Hmm . . . maybe three . . . ?'

Unfortunately, when Maigret looked at him without any emotion or anger, only a touch of irony between his thick eyelids, he lost his footing, stepped back and cast a glance all around him, as if to catch hold of something.

It was a swift transformation. The best he could manage was a coarse smile, which did not keep him from going purple in the face or the pupils of his eyes from shining with anxiety. He had not brought off his act as a *grand seigneur*, so he tried another, more cynical and down to earth.

'That's your bad luck! Anyway, I was being naive – what could you do about it? You have to obey the rules.'

That sounded just as false, and by way of contrast Maigret had probably never conveyed such an impression of quiet, confident power. He was enormous. When he was just below the ceiling light, he touched it with the top of his head, and his shoulders filled the rectangle of the window, in the same way as the lords of the Middle Ages with their huge sleeves fill the frames of old pictures. He was still slowly tidying up the room.

'Because you know I didn't kill anyone, don't you?' said Saint-Hilaire in a fevered tone. He took his handkerchief out of his pocket and blew his nose noisily.

'Sit down,' Maigret told him.

'I'd rather stand . . .'

'Sit down!'

He obeyed, like a frightened child, the moment when the inspector turned to face him. He had a shifty look in his eyes, and the defeated face of a man who does not feel up to his role, and is trying to swim upstream again.

'I imagine,' grunted Maigret, 'that it won't be necessary for me to get the inspector of indirect taxes for Nevers to come and identify his old comrade Émile Gallet? Oh, I'd have worked out the truth without him; it would have taken longer, that's all. I felt for too long anyway that there was something creaky about this story. You needn't try to understand, but when all the material clues manage to confuse matters rather than clarify them, it means they've been faked . . . and everything, without exception, *is* fake in this case. It all creaked. The gunshot and the knife wound. The room looking out on the courtyard and the wall. Severe bruising on the left wrist and the lost key . . . and even the three possible suspects. But most of all Gallet. He sounded as wrong dead as he did living. If the inspector of taxes hadn't spoken up, I was going to go to the school he attended, and I'd have found out the truth there. By the way, you can't have stayed very long at the school in Nantes.'

'Two years! They chucked me out.'

'Good heavens. You were playing football already – and no doubt chasing the girls! Can you hear how the story creaks? Look at this photograph – go on, look at it! At the age when you were climbing the school wall to go and meet your girlfriends, this poor fellow was worrying about his liver. I ought to have devoted some time to collecting the proofs, but I knew what mattered most: my man, who needed 20,000 francs in a hurry, was in Sancerre only to ask you for the money. And you talked to him *twice*! Then, in the evening, you were watching him over the wall! You were afraid he was going to kill himself, am I right? Perhaps he even told you he was?'

'No! But he seemed to me feverish. In the afternoon he was talking in an abrupt tone that made quite an impression on me.'

'And you refused him his 20,000 francs?'

'I couldn't do anything else . . . it was beginning all over again. In the end I think I'd have been broke.'

'It was at your notary's in Saigon that you learned he was going to inherit?'

'Yes . . . an odd sort of client had come to see my boss. An old maniac who'd been living in the sticks for over twenty years, didn't see another white man more than one year in every three. His health was undermined by fevers and opium abuse. I heard their conversation. I'm not long for this world, that's literally what he said, and I don't even know if I have any family somewhere. Could be there's a Saint-Hilaire left, but I doubt it because when I left France the last of them was in such a bad way I guess he's died of consumption. If there's a descendant, and if you can track him down, then he'll be my sole heir.'

'So you already had the bright idea of getting rich at a stroke!' said Maigret thoughtfully. And behind the sweating, ill-at-ease fifty-year-old man before him he thought he could see the unscrupulous jolly companion who organized a grotesque ceremony to get his hands on a young Malay girl.

'Go on.'

'I had to go back to France anyway. It was about women . . . I went too far when I was out there. There were husbands and brothers and fathers who bore me a grudge. So I had the idea of looking for a Saint-Hilaire, and I can tell you it wasn't easy. I picked up the trail of Tiburce at the school in Bourges. They told me they had no idea what had become of him. I knew he was a gloomy young man, reserved, who never had a friend at school . . .'

'Good God!' Maigret laughed. 'He never had a penny in his pocket! There was just enough money to pay for his board until he'd finished his studies.'

'My idea at that moment was to share the inheritance by some means or other, I didn't yet know just how. But I realized it would be harder to share it than to take the lot. It took me three months to lay hands on him, in Le Havre, where he was trying to get taken on as a steward or interpreter on a liner. He had ten or twelve francs left . . . I bought him a drink and then I had to get the information out of him word by word – he never replied except in monosyllables. He'd been a tutor at a chateau, a proof-reader, an assistant in a bookshop . . . he already wore a ridiculous jacket and a strange straggly beard, reddish-brown . . . So I staked everything on getting it all. I told him I wanted to go to America and make my fortune and I said that out there nothing helps a man more, particularly with women, than an aristocratic name, and I offered to buy his. I had a little money, because my father, a horse dealer in Nantes, had left me a small sum of money. I paid 30,000 francs for the right to call myself Tiburce de Saint-Hilaire.'

Maigret cast a brief glance at the portrait photograph, inspected the man he was talking to from head to toe and then looked straight into his eyes in such a way that he began talking at exaggerated speed of his own accord.

'It's what a financier does, isn't it? He buys up securities at 200 francs because he knows he can sell them for five times more a month later. But I had to wait four years to inherit! The old madman out there in his jungle couldn't make up his mind to die. I was the one who almost died of starvation now that I had no money.

'As for the real Saint-Hilaire, we were almost the same age. All we'd had to do was exchange our papers. The other man promised never to set foot in Nantes, where he might have met someone who knew me. As for me, I had to take hardly any precautions. The real Tiburce had never had any friends, and in his various jobs he often didn't use his real name, which didn't sound right for him . . . I mean, how many bookshop assistants are called Tiburce de Saint-Hilaire? Well, at long last I read a little paragraph in the newspapers about the old man's estate and asking anyone with a claim to make himself known. Don't you think I earned the 1,200,000 francs that the old man in the back-woods left?'

He was recovering his self-confidence, encouraged by Maigret's silence, and looked as if he might almost have winked at him.

'Of course, Gallet, who had just got married at that point and wasn't rolling in money, turned up and blamed me for his plight – there was a moment when I thought he was going to kill me. I offered him 10,000 francs, and he finally took them. But he came back six months later . . . and then he came back again. He was threatening to tell the truth. I tried to show him that he'd be thought as culpable as me. What was more, he had a family – and he seemed afraid of that family. Gradually he calmed down . . . he was age-ing fast. I really felt sorry for him with his close-fitting jacket, his beard, his yellow skin and the rings round his eyes. His manner was becoming more and more like a beggar's. He always began by asking me for 50,000 francs – just once and never again, he swore. Then I would fob him off with 1,000- or 2,000-franc notes. But add up those sums over eighteen years! I tell you again that if I hadn't stood firm I'd have been the loser. I was working hard, at that! I was looking for good investments. I planted all the land you see on the higher reaches of the property with vines. While he, on the other hand, was claiming to be a commercial traveller, but the truth was that he was nothing but a scrounger . . . and he got a taste for it. Under the name of Monsieur Clément, as you know, he went around looking for people . . . well, so tell me, what should I have done?'

His voice rose, and automatically he got to his feet.

'So on the Saturday in question he wanted 20,000 francs on the spot. I might have been inclined to give them to him, but I couldn't, because the bank was closed. And then again I'd paid enough, don't you think? I told him so. I told him he was degenerate. He returned to the attack that afternoon, taking such a humble tone that it disgusted me. A real man has no right to let himself sink to such a level as that! A man stakes his life, he wins or he loses, but he keeps more pride than that!'

'Did you tell him that as well?' Maigret interrupted, in a surprisingly gentle voice.

'Why not? I was hoping to stiffen his backbone. I offered him 500 francs.'

Elbows propped on the mantelpiece, the inspector had drawn the portrait photograph of the dead man towards him.

'Five hundred francs,' he repeated.

'I'll show you the notebook where I write down all my expenses. It will show you that at the end of the day he'd got more than 200,000 francs out of me. I was in the grounds that evening . . .'

'And not very much at your ease . . .'

'I was nervous, I can't say why. I heard a noise from beside the wall, and then I saw him fixing I don't know what in the tree. I thought at first he wanted to play some nasty trick on me, but he disappeared just as he had come. When I stood on a barrel for a better look he'd gone into his room, where he was standing upright beside the table, turned to me although he couldn't see me. I couldn't make it out. I swear to you that at that moment I was afraid. The gun went off ten metres from where I was standing, and Gallet hadn't moved . . . only his right cheek was all red, and blood was flowing. But he still stood there staring the same way, as if he was expecting something.'

Maigret took the revolver off the mantelpiece. A guitar string made of several strands of metal, like those you use when fishing for pike, was still tied to it. A small tin box was firmly fixed under the gun and attached to the trigger with a stiff thread.

Opening the box with his fingernail, Maigret found the sort of mechanism you can buy in shops these days allowing you to take a photograph of yourself. All you have to do is load a spring, which releases of its own accord after a certain number of seconds. But in this case the device had a triple movement and so should have set off three shots.

'The spring must have got stuck after the first bullet was fired,' he said slowly, in a rather muted voice. And the other man's last words echoed in his ears: *Only his right cheek was all red, and blood was flowing. But he still stood there staring the same way, as if he was expecting something.*

The other two bullets, for heaven's sake! He hadn't entirely trusted the precision of the device for firing the gun. With three bullets, he was sure of getting at least one of them in his head. But the other two had never gone off! So he had taken his knife out of his pocket.

'He was unsteady on his feet when he pressed its blade against his chest . . . he was straight as he fell . . . dead, of course. The first thing to come into my head was that it was vengeance, that he'd been careful to leave papers revealing the truth, perhaps even accusing me of his murder.'

'You're certainly a prudent man! And talk about a cool head! You went to find rubber gloves in your kitchen . . .'

'You think I was going to leave my fingerprints in his hotel room? I went through the gate and put the key in my pocket. But my visit wasn't any use. He'd burned all his papers himself. I didn't like the look in his open eyes, so I got out of there in such a hurry that I forgot to lock the gate again. Well, what would you have done in my place? Seeing that he was certainly dead . . . I was even more frightened on the day when I was playing cards at the notary's and I learned that the revolver had been fired again. I went to take a look at it, close to, but I didn't dare to touch it, because if anyone got round to suspecting me it was the proof of my innocence. An automatic with six bullets in the chamber . . . I realized that the spring must have stuck after the gun went off, and then slackened again a week late . . . probably because of the atmospheric conditions. But there could still be three bullets left, couldn't there? It's since then that I've spent so much time walking in the grounds, listening for them. Just now, when the two of us were here together, I avoided standing close to the table.'

'But you let me stand there! And it was you who threw the key into the nettle lane when I threatened you with a visit to your home.'

Some of the hotel guests who had finished their dinner were walking along the road. There was an intermittent noise of plates being moved about from the kitchen.

'It was a mistake for me to offer you money . . .'

Maigret almost burst out laughing, and if he had not controlled himself the sound of his laughter would probably have been terrifying. The other man was a head shorter than the inspector, with much narrower shoulders, and standing in front of him, Maigret looked at him with an expression that was both benevolent and fierce, swinging his hand as if to seize him suddenly by the throat or smash his head against the wall.

And yet there was something pitiable about this pseudo Tiburce de Saint-Hilaire, in his desire to justify himself, to regain his self-assurance.

A poor sort of villain, who didn't even have the courage of his villainy, perhaps was not even fully aware of it himself! And he was trying to show off! Every time it looked as if Maigret might move he flinched back. If the inspector had raised his hand he would probably have fallen flat on the floor!

'And by the way, if his wife needs anything I am prepared, discreetly and within my means, to help her.'

He knew he was on safe ground here, but all the same he was not easy in his mind. He'd have given much for a kind word from this police officer, who looked as if he were a cat playing with a mouse.

'He's provided for her himself.'

'Yes, I read that in the papers. Three hundred thousand francs' life insurance! That's extraordinary.'

Maigret could contain himself no longer.

'Extraordinary, isn't it? A man who spent his childhood

without a penny to spend on his small pleasures. And you know what those schools are like. Among the former pupils of the school in Nantes are most of the great men of the centre of the country. He has a fine name. A name as old and lustrous as theirs, apart from that ridiculous first name, Tiburce. But as for him, he may eat and he has a right to have lessons, but he can't buy a chocolate bar or a whistle or marbles . . . At recreation time he's left alone in a corner. Perhaps the poor students paid to supervise the boys take pity on him, they're almost as wretched as he is.

'Well, he gets out of there. He sells books in a bookshop. He hopelessly goes around with his interminable name, his close-fitting jacket, his liver trouble. He has nothing to pawn . . . but he does have that name, and one fine day someone comes along and offers to buy it from him. Without the name, he's still in a miserable state, but with the name of Gallet he can at least attain a higher level: mediocrity. When he is hungry and thirsty, he can eat and drink. But his new family treat him like a mangy dog. He has a wife and a son. His wife and his son blame him for being unable to rise in society, earn money, become a departmental councillor like his brother-in-law. The name he sold for 30,000 francs is suddenly worth a million! The only thing he had possessed, and the one that had brought him most of his wretchedness and humiliation! The name he had got rid of.

'And the man who had really been Gallet, a jolly fellow, good company, gives him alms now and then . . . extraordinary, just as you said. He never succeeded in anything. He spent his life worrying himself sick. No one ever held out a hand to him. His son rebelled and left home as soon as he could to spread his own wings, leaving the old man in his mediocrity. Only his wife was resigned to her situation. I don't say she helped him. I don't say she comforted him. *She was resigned to her situation*, because she realized there was nothing to be done about it. A poor old man on a strict diet.

'And then he leaves her 300,000 francs! More than she ever had when she was married to him. Three hundred thousand francs, enough to make her sisters come running, to win her the smiles of the departmental councillor. He's been dragging himself around for five years, suffering attack after attack of his liver disease. The legitimists don't make him much more than begging would. In these parts he gets his hands on a 1,000-franc note now and then. But there's a Monsieur Jacob, who takes most of what he picks up in that way.

'Extraordinary, yes, Gallet-Saint-Hilaire. Because if he has to cut down on even his small expenses, he keeps up with payments on his life insurance, he spends 20,000 francs a year on it. He senses in advance that a time will come when he finally gives up the ghost, unless his heart is kind enough to stop of its own accord. A poor old man, all alone, coming and going, not at home anywhere unless perhaps when he's out fishing and doesn't see another human being.

'He's born inappropriately, into a family on its uppers that, moreover, has been stupid enough to spend the few thousand francs it has painfully managed to save on his education. He has sold his name inappropriately. And he has worked inappropriately for the cause of legitimism at the moment when legitimism was on its last legs. He married inappropriately – his own son is cut from the same cloth as his sisters- and brothers-in-law. People die every day when they don't want to, when they are happy and well. And he, inappropriately, doesn't die! Life insurance isn't paid if someone has committed suicide. He plays about with watches and springs . . . he knows that the moment when he can't go any further is not far away. And at last, Monsieur Jacob demands 20,000 francs!

'He hasn't got 20,000 francs, and no one will give them to him. He has his spring in his pocket. To put his mind at rest, he knocks on the door of the man who gained a million in his place. He has no hope – and yet he goes back again. But he has already asked for the room looking out on the courtyard, because he is not absolutely sure of his mechanism, and he prefers the simpler option of the well. All his life he has been a grotesque and unlucky figure. And now the room looking out on the courtyard is not available. That means he must climb a wall. And two of the bullets fail to go off. Just as you said: *His right cheek was red . . . blood was flowing. But he still stood there staring the same way, as if he was expecting something.* Hasn't he spent his life expecting something? A little luck? Not even that. One of those little everyday pleasures to be found in the street that people don't notice . . . He had to wait for his two last bullets, and they failed to go off. He had to finish the job for himself.'

The stem of the pipe between Maigret's teeth broke straight off because, as he stopped talking, he had suddenly clenched his jaws. The other man, looking past him, murmured with some difficulty, 'You're right, but all the same he was a crook . . . and for you there's a limitation clause, isn't there?'

'It seems to me that you know the law better than I do.'

'Oh yes, there's a limitation clause. And the law says that there has been no crime or offence when a son lays hands on his father's property by fraudulent means . . . so that Henry Gallet, according to you, has nothing to fear. So far he has only 100,000 francs. With his mistress's fifty, that comes to only 150 and he's going to need 500,000 to go and live in the country as the doctors advise.'

'Just as you said, Monsieur de Saint-Hilaire . . . extraordinary! There's no crime, no murderer, no culprit. There's no one to be sentenced to prison. Or rather, there wouldn't be anyone except my dead man if he hadn't had the bright idea of sheltering from justice under a tombstone in the Saint-Fargeau cemetery . . . made of stone that is *not too expensive, but in good taste and distinguished* . . . Give me a light, will you? Oh, don't worry about using your left hand, *not now*! Come to think of it, there's no reason for you to deny yourself the pleasure of founding a football club in Sancerre any more. You'll be the honorary president . . .'

Suddenly the expression on his face changed, and he said, 'Get out!'

'But I . . .'

'Get out!'

Once again Saint-Hilaire was at a loss. It took him some seconds to regain his composure.

'I think you're exaggerating, inspector. And if . . .'

'Not through the door, through the window. You know the way, don't you? Here . . . you're forgetting your key.'

'When you've calmed down, I'll send you . . .'

'Yes, do that. You can send me a case of the sparkling wine that you got me to taste.'

The other man didn't know whether to smile or be

afraid, but seeing the heavy silhouette of Maigret advancing on him, he instinctively retreated towards the window.

'You haven't given me your address.'

'I'll send it to you on a postcard.'

He abruptly closed the window and was alone in the room, which was bathed in bright light from the electric bulb.

The bed was still just as it had been on the day when Émile Gallet entered this room. His suit of hard-wearing black fabric hung limply on the wall.

With a nervous gesture, Maigret picked up the portrait photo on the mantelpiece, slipped it into a yellow envelope with the letterhead of Criminal Records on it and addressed it to Madame Gallet.

The time was a little past ten. Some Parisian guests who had arrived by car were kicking up a great racket on the terrace, where they had started a portable gramophone playing. They were intent on dancing, while Monsieur Tardivon, torn between his admiration of their luxury car and the complaints of guest who had already gone to bed, was negotiating with the new arrivals, trying to get them into one of the hotel lounges. Maigret went along the corridors, through the café, where a driver was playing billiards with the local teacher, and arrived outside just as a couple dancing the foxtrot suddenly stopped.

'What's he saying?'

'He says his guests have already gone to bed. He wants us to make less noise.'

You could see the two lights of the suspension bridge, and the occasional reflection on the water of the Loire.

'Aren't people allowed to dance?'

'Only indoors.'

'How poetic that would be!'

Monsieur Tardivon, who was primly listening in on this discussion and admiring, with a sigh, the car that belonged to these difficult guests, caught sight of Maigret.

'I've had your place laid in the little salon, inspector. Well . . . is there any news?'

The gramophone was still playing. On the first floor, a woman in a camisole with a scalloped top was watching the newcomers and calling up to her husband, who must be in bed, 'Come down here and make them keep quiet! If we can't even sleep on holiday . . .'

By way of contrast a couple – they looked as if they might be a salesman in a big department store and a typist – were pleading the cause of the new arrivals in their de luxe car, in the hope of getting to know them and spending a more interesting evening than usual here.

'I won't be dining,' said Maigret. 'Would you have my baggage taken to the station, please?'

'For the 11.32 train? Are you leaving, then?'

'Yes, I'm leaving.'

'But all the same . . . you must have something to eat! Do you have our picture postcard of the house?'

Monsieur Tardivon took a postcard with a photo taken twelve years earlier, to judge by the poor reproduction and the women's fashions. It showed the Hôtel de la Loire with a flag hoisted outside the first floor, and the terrace crowded with guests. Monsieur Tardivon was standing in the doorway in morning dress, and the waitresses, holding platters, stood motionless in front of the lens.

'Thank you.'

Maigret put the card into one of his pockets and for a second turned towards the nettle lane.

In the little chateau, a light had just come on at one window, and Maigret could have sworn that Tiburce de Saint-Hilaire was getting undressed and recovering his composure by muttering things like, 'He had to listen to reason, anyway. First of all there's that clause of limitations . . . he could tell that I knew my Roman law as well as he does. And after all, Gallet was nothing but a crook. Come to think of it, what exactly did I do? Yes, what reason is there to blame me for anything?'

But might he not be looking with some alarm at the dark corners of the room?

In Saint-Fargeau, the light must be out in the bedroom where Madame Gallet, her hair pinned up, was divesting herself of anxiety about her dignity, was feeling the empty place between the sheets beside her and perhaps, before going to sleep, was sobbing quietly.

Didn't she have her sisters to console her, and her brothers-in-law, one of them a departmental councillor, all of whom would welcome her back into the comforting bosom of the family?

Maigret had gently pressed the hand of a distracted Monsieur Tardivon as his eyes followed the motorists, who had decided to dine and dance indoors. The suspension bridge, now deserted, echoed beneath his feet, and you could hardly hear the murmur of water running around the sandbanks. Maigret amused himself by imagining a Henry several years older, with an even sallower complexion, his mouth longer and thinner, in the company of Éléonore, her features hardening with advancing age and her figure becoming slightly ridiculous. And they would be arguing. About everything and nothing. But most of all about *their* 500,000 francs – because they would get their money.

'It's all very well for you to talk. Your father was a . . .'

'I won't have you talking about my father . . . and as for *you*, what were you when I first met you?'

'As if you didn't know perfectly well that . . .'

He slept heavily until the train reached Paris, and his sleep was populated by indistinct silhouettes and a nauseating sense of teeming crowds.

When he was about to pay for the coffee laced with something stronger that he drank in the buffet at Gare de Lyon, he took the postcard showing the Hôtel de la Loire out of his pocket. A young girl was sitting beside him eating a croissant and dipping it into a large cup of hot chocolate. He left the card on the zinc counter top. When he turned outside the door, he saw the girl dreamily looking at the end of the suspension bridge and the few trees that framed Monsieur Tardivon's hotel.

Maybe that girl will go there and sleep in the same room, he thought. And Saint-Hilaire, got up in his green hunting garb, will invite her to drink the sparkling wine produced by his estate!

'You look as if you are just back from a funeral,' remarked Madame Maigret, when he came into their apartment on Boulevard Richard-Lenoir. 'Have you at least had something to eat?'

'A funeral . . . yes, you're right,' he said, more to himself than her, looking with pleasure at his familiar surroundings. 'Since he was buried . . .' And he added, although she could not understand, 'All the same I'd rather have a real murder victim and a real murderer . . . Wake me at eleven, will you? I must go and report to the boss.'

He did not confess that he had no intention of sleeping, but he was wondering just what to include in that report.

The truth pure and simple – the truth that would deprive Madame Gallet of those 300,000 francs of life insurance, would set her against her son, against Éléonore, against Tiburce de Saint-Hilaire, and would set her sisters and brothers-in-law against her again?

A tangled skein of clashing interests, of hatreds, of never-ending court cases . . . perhaps a conscientious judge might want to exhume Émile Gallet in order to question him again!

Maigret no longer had the dead man's picture, but he didn't need that faded image now.

His right cheek was all red . . . blood was flowing. He was standing there staring at the same place, as if he was waiting for something.

Peace, for heaven's sake, that's what he was waiting for, growled Maigret, getting up well before the appointed time.

And a little later, shoulders squared, he was telling his superior officer, 'No luck. We can only write off that nasty little case.'

But at the same time he was thinking: the doctor claims he wouldn't have lived three years . . . let's suppose the insurance company loses 60,000 francs . . . it has capital of ninety million.

OTHER TITLES IN THE SERIES

PIETR THE LATVIAN
GEORGES SIMENON

Not that he looked like a cartoon policeman. He didn't have a moustache and he didn't wear heavy boots. His clothes were well cut and made of fairly light worsted. He shaved every day and looked after his hands.

But his frame was proletarian. He was a big, bony man. Iron muscles shaped his jacket sleeves and quickly wore through new trousers.

He had a way of imposing himself just by standing there. His assertive presence had often irked many of his own colleagues.

In Simenon's first novel featuring Maigret, the laconic detective is taken from grimy bars to luxury hotels as he follows a trail of bodies and traces the true identity of the elusive international criminal, Pietr the Latvian.

Translated by David Bellos

OTHER TITLES IN THE SERIES

THE HANGED MAN OF SAINT-PHOLIEN
GEORGES SIMENON

A first ink drawing showed a hanged man swinging from a gallows on which perched an enormous crow. And there were at least twenty other etchings and pen or pencil sketches that had the same leitmotif of hanging. On the edge of a forest: a man hanging from every branch.

A church steeple: beneath the weathercock, a human body dangling from each arm of the cross.

It all started yesterday. Or did it begin years ago? All Maigret knows is that the shabby traveller he was following has committed suicide in a hotel room. As he delves further, a ten-year-old secret begins to emerge – one that some people will do anything to keep.

Translated by Linda Coverdale

OTHER TITLES IN THE SERIES

THE CARTER OF *LA PROVIDENCE*
GEORGES SIMENON

What was the woman doing here?

In a stable, wearing pearl earrings, her stylish bracelet and white buckskin shoes!

She must have been alive when she got there because the crime had been committed after ten in the evening.

But how? And why? And no one had heard a thing! She had not screamed. The two carters had not woken up.

Maigret is standing in the pouring rain by a canal. A well-dressed woman, Mary Lampson, has been found strangled in a stable nearby. Why did her glamorous, hedonistic life come to such a brutal end here? Surely her taciturn husband, Sir Walter, knows – or maybe the answers lie with the crew of the barge La Providence.

Translated by David Coward

OTHER TITLES IN THE SERIES

THE YELLOW DOG
GEORGES SIMENON

There was an exaggerated humility about her. Her cowed eyes, her way of gliding noiselessly about without bumping into things, of quivering nervously at the slightest word, were the very image of a scullery maid accustomed to hardship. And yet he sensed, beneath that image, glints of pride held firmly in check.

She was anaemic. Her flat chest was not formed to rouse desire. Nevertheless, she was strangely appealing, perhaps because she seemed troubled, despondent, sickly.

In the windswept seaside town of Concarneau, a local wine merchant is shot. In fact, someone is out to kill all the influential men and the entire town is soon sent into a state of panic. For Maigret, the answers lie with the pale, downtrodden waitress Emma, and a strange yellow dog lurking in the shadows...

Translated by Linda Asher